The Bells of Christmas

by

Bradley Harper

Erol Engin - Lilla Glass - Will Knight
Derek McFadden - Maria O'Rourke

Compiled and edited by

Jay Lewis Allchin

Copyright 2021

ISBN: 978-1-915221-03-2

This paperback edition compiled by
Papillon du Père Publishing

PAPILLON DU PÈRE
PUBLISHING
Anthology Collections

Books chosen for the *Anthology Collections*
represent our diverse authors

www.papillon-du-pere.com

@PapillonPere

100% of the profits made on the sales of this book will go to *St. Jude Children's Research Hospital*, an organization that helps children to live their best lives.

Cover design

Papillon du Père Publishing

www.papillon-du-pere.com

@PapillonPere

Copyediting

Jay Allchin
@ The Editing-Store.com

www.editing-store.com

STORIES & SPRINKLES

EIGHT STORIES

OF

CHRISTMAS HOPE

Featuring an all-star cast!

Including:

The Bells, Santa Claus, Mrs. Claus, the Ghost of Pops, Young Maria, Old Bear, and even *Sugar Plum* (yes, the fae).

Guest starring *the Soul of Tintoretto* ...

THE BELLS OF CHRISTMAS

BRADLEY HARPER

"I heard the bells on Christmas Day
Their old familiar carols play
And mild and sweet their songs repeat
Of peace on earth, goodwill to men"

The service was ending in the homeless shelter as Salvation Army Captain Agatha led the final carol before the ragged street people crept to bed, full of hot soup as payment for attending Christmas service this bitter night ...

"And in despair I bowed my head
There is no peace on earth, I said
For hate is strong and mocks the song
Of peace on earth, goodwill to men"

There was no peace on earth perhaps, but for these castoffs of society, it would at least reign here until dawn.

Julius burrowed beneath the rough wool blankets as he recalled another Christmas, years ago, when he had his own bed, when a tree with gifts beneath bore his child's name. A broken marriage, alcohol, a son who'd turned away from him in shame, and now a shelter. He'd drifted for many years since, going where the next meal, the next warm place to sleep, would lead.

As I crept past the sleeping forms, his sad dream called to me. I saw that his only surviving wish was to hold his son once more, before his final Christmas, which I knew was but one away. I had a tight schedule, but some things should not be delayed.

I tripped the fire alarm and waited.

The firemen came quickly, in a hail of sirens and lights, and Captain Agatha greeted them when they arrived. "I'm so sorry, gentlemen," she said. "One of our residents must have tripped the alarm bells by mistake. The only warmth here is in the heart."

"Ma'am, I'm required to sweep the premises, all the same," said the fire captain. He walked between the rows of bunk beds, his flashlight sweeping, looking for signs of smoke. His beam lingered on Julius.

"Dad ...?"

> *"Then stirred in bed, his slumber deep*
> *The man alone, his dreams in sleep*
> *Within the light this Christmas night*
> *Some peace on earth, goodwill to men"*

The reindeer snorted when I returned, impatient to get home.

"Hush, hush, Dancer; hush, Prancer. We're done. Our final delivery is complete."

> *"And rang the bells more loud and deep*
> *God is not dead, nor doth He sleep*
> *The wrong shall fail, the right prevail*
> *With peace on earth, goodwill to men"*

THE LAST CHRISTMAS GIFT

DEREK MCFADDEN

I know this is a ride to nowhere. To no*when*, actually.

A ferry ride with no destination. Or, at least, no destination that still exists in the way modern society understands existence. The truth is, I'm trying to find my way back to a place I once knew and loved. A place in which I was always assured of being both known and loved.

"Sweetheart! It's so wonderful to see you! Merry Christmas! Come in, come in! Pop just took a batch of cookies out of the oven, and we bought a new carton of egg nog—just for you because we knew you were coming over!"

My grandmother's greeting plays like a well-loved record in my head. I'm searching for that place this December afternoon, the day before Christmas, in spite of the fact that someone else I don't know owns my grandparents' house now, and they've both been gone almost twenty years. In spite of the fact that, when our ferry reaches the shore, there won't be anyone I love waiting to pick me up. No one to spend Christmas with me. To eat chocolates out of an advent calendar whose dates are marked by a little stuffed-animal mouse you'd move from one date to the next to the next until today's date came to be.

That's because I'm headed for Christmas in the 1990s. A simpler time for me. Likely a simpler time for the world as a whole, but that, I concede, is a broad generalization. It was a time of calm and peace and joy in my life, however, in spite of my cerebral palsy (which turns my right foot too far right and gives people reason to doubt my relevance).

I'm not so much aiming for the *actual* Christmases of the 90s, which—on some level—I know are gone for good. Holidays, by their very nature, are ethereal. Singular moments here one day, gone the next, to stay gone forever. No, I'm searching for the *feelings* those family gatherings left imprinted within me.

Call this a recovery mission.

Nostalgia is what I'm after this early afternoon when no one else appears dumb enough to have paid money to ride a ferry in the middle of a frothy, choppy Puget Sound. An angry Seattle winter rain (is it coming down sideways or is that just my perception?) pelts the otherwise empty boat's windows, the droplets impacting then streaking down the windows out of which I can see little beyond a permanently gray world.

I took this very same ferry ride countless times as a kid. We're talking in the hundreds, maybe even the thousands. Sometimes with my parents. Many times with my younger brother, Ben, four years my junior and the first of us boys to marry the love of his life. (I suppose, in order to marry such a love, you must first find her, a feat I've yet to manage. I thought I'd done it, though, with April.) Many of those sailings were packed full, the car-deck teeming with automobiles and each pair of rectangular seats in the upstairs main cabin filled. So the fact that this ferry is empty, save for its crew—because someone needs to drive this thing and ensure we don't run aground—and I appear to be the only paying passenger aboard is something of a shock to me.

It was my mom who first floated the idea, about a month ago at Thanksgiving, that I board this boat today.

"Why would I do that, Mom?" I asked as we ate too much turkey and watched too much football. "Especially by myself." While I *had* ridden the ferry by myself many times in the past, while I *could* do it, everyone who knew me was well aware I frowned at the thought.

"For old time's sake," my mom said.

Initially, I pushed back against the suggestion. "There's nothing and no one across that water for me, Mom. Not anymore. They're gone."

"They're not gone, Travis. Anyone who still lives within your heart is never truly *gone*."

It was only after having the idea unexpectedly seconded by my therapist, Melody, the following week that I relented.

"I think you should do it!" she said excitedly.

"You what? Why?"

"You may not find your grandparents at the end of that boat ride." On this, she was undoubtedly correct. "But you'll be able to commune with memories and make some new ones while you're at it. I'd wager you'll find some joy in it."

"You'd wager I'll find some joy in it? Do you wanna put your money where your mouth is, Doc?" I challenged.

"It's not *that* kind of wager. But that boat trip is the homework I'm giving you over the holidays, and I expect you to report back and tell me how it went when we see each other again after the New Year."

I left Melody's office, shaking my head and doubting. But taking this ride was my homework. As she said, we'd discuss its effectiveness—along with how many holiday pounds I put on (spoiler alert: too many)—when the calendar flipped to January.

"Enjoy your holidays, Travis!" Melody called after me as I shut her office door behind me.

I'd wondered then if I'd ever actually enjoyed my holidays since my grandparents died. Both of them from cancer. Papa went first, after a six-year-long battle, followed by Grandma, six years later, who lost a battle she kept private until her collapsing in the grocery store meant she couldn't keep the thing that would end her private any longer.

On this nearly empty boat (it's *too* empty! This same short voyage was packed full of souls on past holidays—I saw it with my own not-great eyes), I again question the wisdom of this "assignment."

I take a seat on one of the many available bench-seats. Ferry boat etiquette dictates that no one will sit either with or on the seat across from anyone they don't know, which means this pair of bench-seats is all mine for the next twenty minutes. As I settle onto the soft bench and gaze out the window at a quintessential pacific northwest Christmas—the sky dark with clouds pouring rain—the usual perfunctory announcements I've heard a thousand times crackle over the vessel's loudspeaker. Which is garbled and staticky and not all that loud.

Life preservers at the front and back of the boat, if needed (sure hope we never, ever need them). Follow all crew instructions (as if I was planning to mutiny on Christmas Eve!). Enjoy your ride from Edmonds, Washington, across the Puget Sound to the small town of Kingston. (Okay, so this last announcement wasn't quite as involved as I've written it; all they said was, "Enjoy the sailing," but a writer needs to fit exposition in somewhere.)

This isn't my first Christmas without my grandparents. It's not even the first Christmas I'll technically spend alone. I'm no introvert, trust me, so it's not like I *want* to spend it alone, but convincing people to hang with you on Christmas is a tough ask, especially when they don't have a connection to you beyond the workplace, or maybe they're an acquaintance with whom you're friendly but distant, as society requires these days. But this is the most conspicuous of all of my "alone" Christmases for one simple reason: I'm going through a break-up.

Writing that little phrase takes real guts. Guts I haven't had until now. That's right, I've been trying to admit this truth to myself for two months now: *I'm going through a break-up.* But it's refused recognition. Or, more accurately, my mind wouldn't allow it to cross the necessary synapses in my brain and *be* recognized.

As the reality of the break-up began to dawn on me six months ago (this was, after all, a process), I considered therapy for the first time. Not physical therapy, mind you—of which I've had more than my share, born as I was with cerebral palsy and a body inherently wound tight—I'm talking about the kind of therapy one gets when things don't feel right ... upstairs.

I first met my therapist, Melody, on a Tuesday afternoon.

"So what brings you here, Travis?" she'd asked, looking at me over a pair of big glasses.

At that exact moment, I didn't really know. Or, if I knew, I didn't want to say.

"I love my girlfriend, and she suggested I get into therapy."

"Ah. What's her name?"

"April."

"Is she in counseling, too?"

I nodded. "She thinks I could get a lot out of it. So I'm here."

Melody leveled her gaze directly at me for the first time. "And what do *you* think?"

"What do I ...?"

"Think? Yes, what do you think? Is April right?"

"I hope so. Otherwise, I don't know what I'm doing here."

Hearing this fact escape my mouth brought a twinge to my chest, and I didn't know why.

"Travis, what do *you* want and expect out of our time together?" Melody challenged me.

"I don't know," I lied.

"Yes, you do," she pressed. "I suspect you do know, or you wouldn't be here. What do *you* want?"

"I want to go back in time," I said after a long moment.

"How's that?" Melody removed a pencil from behind her ear and wrote something on a pad of paper to her right. Something, I imagine, like, *Has grandiose but impossible ideas about life.* "Why do you want to go back in time?"

"Because ..." I thought about it. "Because there was a time when people loved me, and that time has *clearly* passed, and I'd like to get back to it. I want to go back in time. You understand, don't you, Doc?"

"I understand you might not feel good right now, Travis. But we'll work on fixing that. It'll take time and effort on both our parts, but we'll fix it. Together. But to get there means your cooperation. This won't work unless you give me your complete cooperation. Do I have it?"

You either do this, and do it right, or April will leave you, I'd thought back then. That couldn't happen. "You have it, Doc," I agreed.

I've been seeing Melody twice a week ever since. Yet, as helpful as my counseling has been, it *did not* and *cannot* save my relationship. April is gone. Has been for about a month or so now. We keep saying we'll find time to celebrate "our" Christmas together, but I know I won't see her until the New Year at the earliest.

Effectively, I'm holding onto something that is no longer a *something.*

The ship has sunk. And I'm its loyal captain, duty bound to go down with my doomed charge.

Taking the advice of both my mom and my therapist, I board a boat I've likely been on countless times (although, who's to say? All these vessels look the same, and it's difficult for me to read the name affixed to the vessel's front both because my eyes are not—and never have been—good, and on account of the wind-blown mist-rain that acts as a spray this winter day, buffeting me as I enter the cabin), I'm going back in time. In a manner of speaking, anyway. Or at least as far back in time as modern technology will allow me to go.

Thinking back on all the Christmases I spent with my grandparents, something else Melody has asked me to do as a kind of homework, I realize only now that I don't remember each holiday as a distinct entity. As much as I'd like to, I don't. Rather, they run together; one runs into the next, which runs into the Christmas after it. It is as though my usually unimpeachable memory, in an attempt to catalogue everything—from Papa's refrigerator cookies to the playing of Stan Borreson records (a uniquely *us* Christmas tradition important only to our family) to Grandma's intentionally bad carol-singing to my favorite Christmas gifts of all time—in an attempt to remember it all, my memory has abridged my holidays. And, in only recording the basics, my memory has squandered what it was about Christmas that once made the holiday essential.

Or maybe I'm just getting older and the things that mattered to me when I was a kid just don't matter anymore. Maybe it's that simple.

My thoughts can't help but return to the emptiness of this boat. An emptiness I might understand if this sailing came early in the morning. But smack in the midst of a cold afternoon, I don't get it.

I should be here with April, I think. If she were here, everything would be different. Better.

I'm glancing out the window as this thought occurs to me. Maybe I should refute it, but I'm too tired to try. A break-up takes a lot out of a guy.

"So you're feeling sorry for yourself? That's what you're doing now? On Christmas Eve, of all days?"

I *know* that voice. Only one man could ever speak to me in such a cutting yet insightful manner.

I turn from the window ...

To see my papa.

A young version of my papa—still sporting the black hair of my early childhood, hair that has yet to turn silver—is sitting across from me on an otherwise empty close-to-yellow bench-seat. He's wearing a plaid shirt under a "Kiss-The-Cook" apron. Not exactly ferry-riding clothing, but at least it fits the holiday. I'd be willing to bet there's a bottle of Tums either in a pocket of his blue jeans or stowed inside the winter coat that he wears, unzipped. ("It's not *that* cold," he'd often say.)

Is he really sitting there, or am I just overtired?

"Pop?"

"Yeah, it's me."

"How?"

"How isn't important," he says, looking me straight in the eye, the intensity of his gaze off-putting. Papa only ever looked at me this way when he was trying to hammer home a point I'd failed to grasp, or when he thought I was doing something *very* wrong and he needed to step in.

""I feel so alone," I say.

"Uh-huh," Pop says, but what he's really saying without saying it is: *What does that mean to you?*

I don't respond to this unasked question. Instead, I say something to my papa that I never thought I'd get to say again. "Merry Christmas, Pop."

Just this phrase chokes me up. I fight to keep the tears from coming. Swallow down the lump in my throat.

"Merry Christmas, kid." He pauses, changes the subject. "I think we've got work to do."

"How's that? I mean, how can that be?"

"*How* I'm here is not important," Pop explains. "What's important is *why*."

I'm thrown off. I don't know why. Other than I'd definitely thought that, the next time I saw Pop, gone nearly two decades now, the next time I wished him a Merry Christmas, the mood would be celebratory. We'd be reunited to stay.

"Okay ... so, why are you here, Pop?" I ask.

"I'm here because you need me. But let's not worry about that just yet. Tell me about your life."

"Tell you about my life?"

"Yeah. What have I missed since I've been gone? Tell me all of it." He takes from his coat pocket a folded section of his newspaper. "And, while you talk and I listen, I've got a crossword to do. I hope you don't mind if I interrupt you if I have any questions for you. Or if I get stuck on a clue."

Strange. But okay: after all, why disagree when your long-dead grandfather shows up on Christmas Eve and tells you he's shown up because you need him? Foolhardy to argue the point! These parameters agreed to, I begin the story of my life since his passing, and Pop begins his puzzle as he'd always begun every one of his crossword puzzles: hopeful.

Pop, the man who taught me how to swim over many successive summer vacations—"Kick your feet, Travis! You're handicapped, but you still *have* legs. Don't forget about 'em. Use 'em. Kick those feet!"— and the man who taught me how to love without ever *trying* to teach me how to love—*Treat every girl I date the way Pop treated Grandma, I'll be fine*, I remember thinking on many a date—the man I thought could never die because heroes never died ... that man passed away when I was just a week shy of my twenty-first birthday. Back then, my life was infinite and limitless as it stretched out before me. *Sure, I might be handicapped, but I can do anything I put my mind*

to. I won't be climbing a mountain anytime soon, mind you, I thought. *But that's never been a dream of mine, anyway. The things I want to do, whatever those things end up being, I will do.* My parents, and especially my paternal grandparents, had hammered this idea home for years. In the years immediately prior to Pop's passing, it was taking hold.

Since then, I've learned the truth.

And I've learned that the truth hurts.

"I don't know where to start, Pop," I tell him, my head in my hands.

He doesn't look up from his crossword, which he's donned his glasses to read. "Start at the beginning. That way, you can tell the whole story." Though he's still looking at the newspaper, now I can glimpse the hint of a smile playing on his mustachioed lips.

"Okay. Well, first thing's first, Pop. It hasn't all been great since you've been gone."

Now he places the crossword facedown on his lap. Looks into my eyes. "You think if your life was running smoothly, Travis, that I'd be here right now? Tell me from the beginning. If I have questions, I'll cut in and ask them. But you're a writer, aren't you?" I *had* published a novel about a year ago. If doing so made you a writer, then I *was* a writer. "All writers are storytellers. Tell me your story," he repeats, firmer this time.

Alright, I think. *From the beginning.*

"Pop, you died on a Saturday in May, only a week before my twenty-first birthday. I don't know why, maybe it's out of some sort of morbid curiosity, but ever since, I've wondered on what day of the week I would die. That twenty-first birthday was the saddest birthday I've ever experienced. That first beer I'd been waiting to have with you and its accompanying steak didn't taste too good because, even though Dad was there, you weren't, Pop.

"After you died, Pop, Grandma got mean. I'm sure you were watching, so you had to see it, but she went from the happy-go-lucky Grandma I knew to a suddenly sour, self-centered wench. I'm sorry. I know you love her, and we're not supposed to speak ill of the dead, but it's the truth."

At this, Pop nods in acknowledgment. *Proceed,* the gesture says, as he grunts his disapproval with one of his puzzle's more difficult clues.

I go on. Speaking of this particular time of year, I tell Pop how Christmas, formerly my favorite holiday, was never the same after he passed. Grandma did her best, of course. Our whole family did. But when someone dies in a family, and especially when that someone was the glue that kept a family together, there's only so much *anyone* can do to hold together a now-tattered quilt of relations. Within a couple years, the tradition of holding Christmas Day at Pop and Grandma's house ended. It did so unceremoniously. No one came right out and said, "This is the last year we're doing Christmas here." Had someone actually said this, in as many words, I'm confident an outcry would have resulted. Instead, it was never directly discussed; we just knew we didn't want to spend an hour or more in a ferry line every December 25th, and my dad has spent every Christmas since hosting a subsection of the large crowd who used to congregate at Grandma and Papa's place.

Now Pop looks annoyed. I stop talking a second.

"What's wrong, Pop?" I ask.

"Two things," he grumbles. "First of all, I don't need a history lesson on our family."

"You don't?"

"No. I was in it before you were. What I need is for you to be honest with yourself."

"About what?"

"About what it is you're actually doing on this boat." He pauses, fixes me with a look that says, *You can lie to yourself, Travis, but you better not lie to me.* "And second," he continues, "I need your help."

"With what?"

"With this damn clue. I can't make heads or tails of it. Four across. The clue is *bathday cake,* whatever the hell that means. S, blank, blank, blank."

Ah, he's mad at his crossword, too. I've seen him work many a crossword before, and he's continually furrowing his brow at this one. I honor Pop's second request first because it's the easiest to carry out. "Soap," I tell him.

"Soap?"

"Yeah, you know ... like a cake of soap."

"Boy, you are pretty smart, aren't you?" He pencils this in and smiles when he realizes it works.

"I like to think so," I say.

"So then, what the hell are you doing on this boat?"

I sit back, letting myself sink into the bench-seat, and consider this. "I don't know. I'm depressed—"

"That much is obvious."

"I'm *depressed.*" I'm talking louder now, and I've made sure to emphasize the word. It isn't merely a word or simply a state I've been mired in recently. The fact is, depression is now one of the major tenets of my personality. I hate it, but I can't seem to escape it.

"Shit, we've all been depressed. You think when I was in Korea, scared shitless, that I wasn't also goddamned depressed? 'Course I was. Could have been home with my young family on Christmas, for example, but instead I was half a damn world away contemplating the killing of other human beings. How, if I didn't kill them, they might well kill me."

"Jeez, Pop, if you don't want me to tell you the story of my life since you've been gone—"

"I *do* want you to tell me that story. But I want you to start from *your* beginning and focus on what matters most to *you*. This is only a twenty-minute boat ride, after all."

I lean forward, placing my hands on my knees. "Okay ... okay. So, I'm not sure what matters to me anymore, Pop. I used to know. I used to be *certain* of what mattered to me. But then ..."

"But then what?" Pop pencils in a crossword answer as I begin to wonder, *What is this?* My papa returned to human form on a magical Christmas Eve, or is it simply another session with Melody?

"But then April gave up on me. On us."

"Your relationship ended, is what you're saying?"

"Yeah. That's right."

Maybe he'd oversimplified the thing. April and I had a vibrant and varied history together, from our trips to Disneyland to the many times we'd held each other up when one or the other of us was ruled by feelings we didn't fully understand. Be they depression, manic joy, or apprehension and anxiety. But he *is* right. My relationship has ended. Even admitting this much stirs my feelings like a chef would stir an indigestible, unwanted pot of soup. Not Pop's, though, my favorite chef of all time; he liked to make turkey soup for the holidays. And we loved consuming it.

"What do you want, Travis? For the world to feel sorry for you?" he challenges.

"No, no, I don't want that. What I want is ..." I pause, and only then do I realize I've misspoken.

"Okay, so maybe I do want the world to feel *a little* bad for me. To realize what I had and how ... how *good* it was. And all I had to go through to get it! And how sad I am that it's gone forever."

"That's asking an awful lot of the world," Pop says. There's no judgment in his tone. But there *is* honesty. "And, truthfully ..." He reaches into his coat pocket and extracts a Tums tablet, something I'd seen him do so many times in life; heartburn enjoyed shadowing him. "Truthfully, it's asking an awful lot of yourself, too. Nostalgia is one thing. I'm all for a trip into the past. But when you take those trips, you have to be absolutely clear-eyed about where and when it is you're going and what your objective will be once you get there. What it is you *want*."

Pop was so good at this. He'd always been so good at this. The taking aside of his grandchildren and, honestly, anyone who was his charge, and telling them—always quietly, so as not to embarrass them, but always dead-straight, and right when they needed to hear it—how life worked. Before my brother and I, he'd done the same for my father and my uncle. And my older cousins, my uncle's kids, the eldest of whom is a decade my senior. Neither of us is kids anymore.

"The whole world can't stop and mourn a lost relationship with you. The world stops for absolutely no one; that's the same thing your grandmother wanted when she lost me—and she didn't get it, either. So what is it you really want, kid?" He's looking at me purposefully over his glasses.

"I want to know what it feels like not to have my cerebral palsy! I'm always walking in molasses. Other people move around with a confidence and a freedom I'll never know."

"Did I say I was a genie, Travis?"

"What? No."

"Then why would you continue to ask me for things I can't give you? I'm here to *help* you. Not to transform your life into some unrealistic fantasy. We each are given the life we're given. That's what we get. No more, no less. And, sure, people complain about their lots in their lives all the time. It's natural, part of being human. You ever known anyone able to do what you're asking?"

I think hard, my head resting against the back of my bench-seat. All the while knowing the answer is no. "What about rags to riches stories? They happen all the time."

Pop gives me a look that says, *You're kidding me, right?* He doesn't need to actually say that if I'm not gonna take this seriously, he'll go back to his crossword.

"Well, they happen all the time in the movies," I correct.

"Is your life a movie?"

"No."

Sometimes, I might *want* to be in a movie, though. The charming star. I won't lie. Specifically, in one of those romantic comedies where the good guy—me, of course—always gets the girl in the end, and the biggest problem the couple has on their path to matrimonial and forever-after bliss is when the absent-minded guy forgets he's made a date with his beloved and inadvertently stands her up waiting for him at a fancy restaurant, leading to the twenty minutes in the film during which our guy thinks he's lost the girl for good, only to find out that, no, he hasn't. And he *won't.* Because it's a movie, the modern equivalent of a fairy tale, and Hollywood demands its heroes succeed, by any means necessary. Meaning that, no matter how much of a failure I feel like in real life, I couldn't fail in a movie.

"You trying to live a movie? Even though, Mr. Writer, you know your life isn't one?"

I don't want to tell him my reasoning, which I've just come by, and of which I'm not proud. He won't like it. *I* don't like it. So I stay quiet. Let him get to his point.

"Don't live a movie. Live the moment."

"Live the moment?" I say, skepticism reigning in both my voice and my countenance.

He nods.

"And how do I do that? I've never even heard that expression before. Unless you mean live *in* the moment?"

"I don't," Pop answers. "I said what I meant to say. *Live the moment.* It means to accept each moment in life as it comes. To live *that* moment's reality in full. Don't get ahead of it. Try not to lag behind it. When another moment comes, only then do you move into that moment and live *its* reality."

As what he says soaks in, I glance out the window. A dread is prickling at the back of my neck. The same dread I felt when I *knew* April was about to end things. But this dread is upon me for an entirely new reason.

I can still barely see anything out the boat window. All I know for certain is how the trees on the shore we'll reach in another ten minutes or so are getting closer and closer. My time with Papa, whom I haven't seen in so, so long, is ebbing away, sifting through my fingers like the finest grains of white sand on the Hawaiian beach he always wanted to visit but never did. Never could. (Grandma brought his ashes with us on the trip we took after his death, and she spread about a quarter of them on that beach, in that saying, "He made it to Hawaii after all.")

"See, you're not doing it," Pop admonishes, and his gruff voice has me leaving Hawaii, and I'm back on the boat on a rainy Christmas Eve.

"Not doing what?"

"You're not living the moment, Travis. You're not here with me now. Hell, you're not even on this boat. You're thinking about Hawaii and how your grandmother spread my ashes on the beach because I'd asked her to, and how I wasn't there—I was there, by the way, you just couldn't see me—and how it hurt you that I wasn't there."

I can't deny it. Any of it. He knows. *Just as he always seemed to know when I was "fibbing," my grandmother would call it.* I nod. Hide my face. I don't want him to see how tears are collecting at and stinging the backs of my eyes.

I can't let them fall.

"I'm so lonely," I admit to my grandfather. The admission shocks me. I hadn't known I was going to fess up to my loneliness until the three-word phrase was well clear of my mouth, its gatekeeper the last six months or so. That phrase has wanted out for half a year but not been granted leave until now.

Being lonely is different than being alone. Worse, harder to admit.

"How come?" Pop asks. "Why are you so lonely?"

"All the people I love ... What's the point of loving people the way I do? Holding them close over the holidays? Holding them close in my heart *all the time?* Giving them my *whole* heart the way I do? All the people I love eventually leave me. And there's nothing I can do about it."

"Welcome to life, kid," Pop declares, without actually declaring *anything.*

It's the most matter-of-fact I've ever seen him. This man who loved to joke. Sarcasm ran in tandem with the blood in his veins. This was a man who, on a snipe hunt he himself organized one summer Saturday night for my brother and me, looked me dead in the face and told me he'd just seen a snipe, a real-life *snipe*, and when I said I hadn't seen it, he swore it *was right there*. I'd simply been looking the other way, the *wrong* way, and he hadn't managed to get my attention fast enough. Before the animal—which I, of course, didn't know was imaginary at the time— skittered away, back into its burrow.

Yes, Pop loved to joke. Which meant that when he fell into his *serious* mode, you stopped what you were doing and you listened. That's what my brother and I would do, anyway. Pop had us well trained.

"Did all the people you love leave you, too, Pop?" I ask him.

"No."

"See, I *knew* it. It's me. There's something wrong with me. Beyond the palsy, I mean. Something's *really* wrong. That's why people lea—"

"No," Pop continued, ignoring my interruption. "Everyone I love didn't leave me. Because sometimes ... sometimes, *I* had to leave them, even though I didn't want to, and even though the leaving hurt like hell."

Marked by black pilings, the dock looms mere minutes ahead. My time with Pop is drawing to a close. But it doesn't appear he has much more to say to me. He goes back to his crossword.

Giving all he's said the time it needs to sink in?

Only when he finishes the puzzle does he take off his glasses, put them back in his coat pocket, toss the newspaper section down on the seat next to him, and sigh deeply.

"I suppose I should ask you now," he says, "what it is you need from me?"

"What I *need* from you?"

"Sure. You think dead grandfathers appear to their living grandsons every day? *Sheesh!* That would merit some news coverage. I'm *here* because you need something from me. Haven't you figured that out already?"

I'm embarrassed to tell him I hadn't.

Above us, the ferry's not-so-great loudspeaker crackles back to life. "We are arriving at our destination. All passengers *must* disembark the vessel within five minutes. Thank you."

By all passengers, I guess that guy means me. Who else is there?

So, what *do* I need from Pop?

"When April told me we were done," I explain, "I hadn't expected it, though all the signs of a relationship in trouble and fracturing had been there—how she'd been pulling away from me, and everyone could see it *but* me, because I chose not to see it—I remember one thought dominated my mind."

"What thought was that, Travis?

"How, if April only knew what my papa was like. How he'd raised me to believe in myself but not to be cocky, to *appreciate* my disability—instead of seeing it as a constant disadvantage, the reason I *couldn't* do things. And how he'd taught me to live every moment as though it was the most important moment of my life, because each succeeding moment *is* the most important moment of my life ... That's what it means to live in the present ... Guess I lost sight of that a little. But if April could only know all of these things about the man who made me a man, she wouldn't be breaking up with me." I pause. Gather my few belongings. I didn't bring many things with me besides myself. But in this post-9/11 world, we're trained as a society to scan our spaces and make certain both that we aren't leaving anything behind and that *no one else* has left anything in their wake, either.

I sigh. Even as I say all that ... I know it's not exactly true. "Even if April knew you, Pop, even if she'd loved you as deeply as I did, *as I always will*, I s'pose we would still have ended the way we ended."

"You think? Why's that?" Pop rose to his feet with me, his newspaper in the crook of his arm.

"I guess relationships only work if two people are willing to do the work. Together. And I guess maybe I had trouble living the moment. I've had trouble with that sort of thing since forever. I've always looked ahead. To the next milestone in our relationship, the next big vacation. Our next dinner-and-a-movie date. That next trip to Disneyland."

"And April?"

"April was dealing with her own stuff. Anxiety. Which induced panic. Which brought on sickness. Which is why she couldn't live the moment, either. I wanted to help her, to be there for her in the way I thought I was supposed to, as a man, but ..." I couldn't say the rest. It hurt too much to admit.

"But what?" Pop pushes.

"But the way I give support ... gave support ... maybe it wasn't the particular kind of support April needed. I may never know what it was she needed ... not precisely, anyway. All I know is ... as much as I wanted to, I couldn't give it to her."

At this, I wobble on my feet. Stagger back. Reach for Pop's considerable girth, hug him around his belly, and I begin to sob.

"I didn't want it to end, Pop," I cry. "I didn't want *us* to end."

"No one ever does *want* endings, kid," Pop says. "No one ever does."

As I speak these words, my soul begins to lighten, a massive invisible weight lifting. The relationship is over, but it's not my fault. *It's not anyone's fault.* It just is. From now on, as best I can, I'm going to live the moment; not three moments ahead or five moments behind.

Out the window, a cloudy sky is beginning to truly darken. It's 4 p.m. The sun has exited on cue, and somewhere near the North Pole, Santa must be readying his goodie-laden sleigh for a long but well-planned flight. It occurs to me that Santa would know how to live in the moment. At the same time, my surroundings inside the boat begin to change. To transform. There's been no one aboard this boat for our entire short voyage; now the bench-seats around me fill with families eager for the coming holiday.

"What the ...?" I'm taken aback by the sudden appearance of others. "Where did all these people come from, Pop?"

"These people?" Pop smiles, sweeps his hand over the greater area in much the same way a model on his favorite gameshow, *The Price Is Right*, might if she were showing off a new car. I still watch that show. Not every day but most days. Precisely because he loved it. "These folks've been on this boat the whole time."

"Then how come I couldn't see them? Pop, the boat was empty. I'd swear to that fact under oath, counselor," I say, doing my best imitation of a frazzled witness on one of the many police procedurals that populated the TV landscape in Pop's day, and still do.

"Most people are only focused on themselves."

I look around. "And their phones."

"Same thing, some would argue. Either way, they don't see you. For you, it isn't a phone that's blocking the world." He's right. I'm the one person on this planet who still doesn't have a phone. "It's you—your turmoil, Travis. Until you could clear the turmoil in your mind, you weren't going to see any of these people."

We prepare to disembark. I'm in line behind a little girl of about eight and her parents, who are each carrying a not-so-small pile of gift-wrapped packages. The little girl begins to sing. Softly at first. But as she gains confidence, her voice grows louder. And, as the rest of us realize what's happening, we join her. An impromptu caroling session that started with Jingle Bells, and by the time the boat's crew has the doors open and we're exiting in earnest, we're on to Let It Snow.

When that second song finishes, Pop is in my ear again. "You know I can't go any further, right?"

"What?"

"This isn't my world anymore. It's yours now, Travis. As long as you live the moments as they come, you'll be just fine."

"No!" I want to cry. Not again! I can't lose my papa *again*. I want to cry, scream my protest. But I know it'll do no good. Pop has to go. I know it. He's come to help me, but his Christmas delivery has now been made.

I look to the sky and see the cold rain has been replaced by soft snow. Just as the little girl and we carolers had asked. *Did Papa do this?*

"Merry Christmas, kid." His last words to me fade on the breeze and the flurry of snowflakes dancing around me.

"Merry Christmas, Pop. Thanks for showing me what I was missing. Thanks for setting me straight."

Since I had to disembark—I had no choice—I decided to walk from the ferry dock up a few blocks and then ascend the steep hill leading to my grandparents' old house ...

Where I'd spent so much of my childhood.

Where I'd been so loved and appreciated.

But when I got to the house, what I saw wasn't *their* house. It wasn't the house where I'd spent so many Christmases, so many summers, so many late afternoons sleeping in, only to mock-annoy Papa with the news that I wanted him to make me breakfast. His rule was the kitchen closes at 10 a.m. Somehow, I always managed to get my order in around 9:58.

Which always made my grandmother smile. "He's not late, Dick," she'd say. "He got his order in on time."

I loved *that* house. But it isn't *that* house anymore. It's just a dwelling. Someone else's domicile. Where someone else's memories are being made now. Where *their* family will spend holidays and seasons.

I still have memories to make, I think. So many memories. *They just ... won't be made here.*

And that's okay.

With this thought, I turn and make my way back to the ferry dock for the short trip home, aware of the last Christmas gift my grandfather will ever give me. Aware that, though I cannot hold it in my hands, his gift is more valuable than any material possession ever could be. And I'll forever hold it deep in my heart.

Derek McFadden
Bio

Derek McFadden is an author, a poet, a radio enthusiast, an unapologetic fan of the Seattle Mariners, and a former March of Dimes ambassador. Derek lives with a mild version of cerebral palsy, and his eyes aren't great at being eyes.

Derek's acclaimed novel *What Death Taught Terrence* was a Next Generation Indie Book Award Finalist and is available in hardcover, paperback, e-book, and Audible editions. His short story, *What Eternity Taught Eve*, featured in Papillon du Père's anthology ***13 by 11*** and included an appearance from the main character of his novel.

Find Derek's books at

Amazon

Visit Derek on

Facebook

A WINTER CANDLE

BRADLEY HARPER

"If you save one life, it is as though you saved
the world entire."

– The Talmud

*There are many kinds of stories. Some are true, some are
make-believe, and some are left for you to decide.
I'll tell you this story just the way Santa told it to me. I
believe it's true, because Santa never lies.*

One

It was a June afternoon in San Antonio, Texas, and too hot for even the turkey vultures to fly, huddling together in the live oak trees on the border of the parade ground, looking like a cluster of small Greek widows. Ben and twenty-five other "old soldiers" wearing their dress uniforms were gathered in the shade of the awning adjoining the field, sitting on hard metal chairs while waiting for their name to be called. The post Adjutant General was standing upon the podium beside a low table with their retirement certificates neatly lined up in alphabetical order, ready to hand the honorees a ticket to a new life, or at least a hard shove from the old.

Ben knew which category he fell into and wondered if the Army ever had to execute more than one prisoner on the same day if it would be done in alphabetical order. He had tried to skip the ceremony but was told attendance was mandatory, and now as the sweat trickled down his forehead, he craned around to look for anyone who had come to witness his final act as an army officer. Anyone at all.

The young soldiers in formation in the sun looked bored and miserable, as Ben knew he had looked when he'd stood at attention for similar ceremonies. As the time passed, he went from standing in the rear to the front of the troops, which only meant he had to stay erect longer. At least this time he got a chair in the shade.

Finally, his name was called, and he did his best not to look at the crowd. But once he was on the stage, he couldn't keep himself from one last sweep. The silence as he climbed the steps told him what his eyes confirmed.

The presiding officer mumbled the same platitudes he'd heard all the other times, reaffirming Ben's impression that he was an easily replaceable cog in a huge machine. He'd been a logistics officer, so the concept of interchangeable parts was familiar to him.

Families and friends surged forward for hugs and photographs once the echoes of the final song faded away, marking the end of the ceremony and his twenty-four-year career. As he watched the young troops march away, grateful for their release, he knew that the Army would be just fine without Lieutenant Colonel Ben Fuller, Logistics Corps.

No, no question about that.

He thought back to the day he was promoted to captain, how impressed Emily had been with the two silver bars, his "railroad tracks" on his collar, and how sergeants began to act as though he knew what he was talking about. He'd promised her that day that even if he made general, if she wasn't there the day he retired he'd feel a failure.

He knew she remembered that conversation as well as he did. Her absence as he trudged alone to his twelve-year-old car was a final reckoning of their failed marriage, and of the failed man she'd married. A program from the ceremony drifted by on a feeble breeze, and Ben picked it up without thinking and detoured to the trash bin at the corner of the parking lot. He threw the program in, then after looking at the one he'd been issued when he arrived, added it and went back to his car, empty-handed.

After he started the old Volvo and rolled down the window to allow some of the Texas heat to vent, his shirt pocket vibrated. He pulled out his phone to see a text, and he almost smiled when he saw who it was from. *Happy retirement Big Brother*, the text read. *Sorry I couldn't make it there from California. Now that you're a free man, you should come here. Your nephews miss you, and yeah well, maybe I do too. Celebrate tonight, you earned it! Susan.*

He sighed. Trips cost money. *Maybe next year*, he thought, knowing he'd said that too many times about too many things.

He cruised to the trailer park and the doublewide he now called home, the radio off, his memories of years in uniform forming the backdrop to the listless drive. He had one month's leave when he would still draw full pay; after that, his monthly payment would shrink to sixty percent of his base salary. After alimony, child support, and the loss of his housing allowance, Ben had one month before his personal income would shrink by seventy-five percent. His plan for a nice government-contracting job or as a manager in a mid-size company dried up with his DUI and the loss of his security clearance. His requests for letters of recommendation from former commanding officers were either ignored or flatly denied.

Ben looked in the mirror before he took his uniform off for the final time.

"Time to right-size your expectations, Colonel," he said to his reflection.

He paused and looked at the closet where his uniform with all its ribbons and campaign medals would hang, probably until he was buried in it, and wondered who he was without the identity he'd been issued along with his uniform.

The closet offered no answers.

Like most men, Ben didn't see the divorce coming. The nights he'd stayed late, the dinners and birthdays he'd missed because he'd volunteered for this or that mission—hoping to impress his superiors—had, like barnacles on a ship, steadily slowed their relationship. The last couple of years, they could go a week without having a complete conversation. Emily said she was tired of her and Daniel, their now ten-year-old son, being an afterthought. When Ben got passed over for promotion the third and final time, he began drinking too much and shoved his wife and son away as he nursed his sense of betrayal with a brown bottle.

His DUI was the final straw: Ben lost his driver's license for six months, so Emily had to chauffeur him around between taking Danny to soccer practice, school, and going to her job as a realtor. The day his license was restored was the day she left a note on the breakfast table, saying she had taken Danny to her mother's for the weekend and she wanted him out when they came back. There was also a letter from a lawyer.

The end of his twenty-year marriage was even less ceremonious than his army career. He didn't fight it. Why would he? What man forces a woman to live with him? He got visitation rights two weekends a month, but, so far, Danny had refused to come. Emily hadn't seemed interested in forcing the issue, and as Ben looked around the doublewide he asked himself why his son would want to. He had no video game system, couldn't afford cable, and the bedroom Danny would use was barely more than a closet.

The only thing of Danny's he'd brought with him was a fishing rod, never used. A reminder of a trip Ben had kept delaying until it was now too late. Ben had it and his own ancient rod stacked together in a corner of the sitting area, trophies of sorts to his record of broken promises.

He'd tried to go to Daniel's soccer games, but the first time he went his son recognized him and left the field, refusing to go back out until Ben left. Emily came over, blushing from the looks of the other parents. "Please, Ben. Danny doesn't want to see you. I know you want to stay part of his life, and I respect that. He's just not ready yet."

Ben nodded, did an about-face turn any drill sergeant would approve of, and slunk off to his car, feeling the eyes of the entire sideline on his back. He didn't dare imagine what scenarios they had playing in their heads. And he didn't care to stick around to find out.

He tried one more time, staying well back, but Danny picked him out of the crowd and Ben went straight to his car before Danny headed off the field.

He'd dreamt of his retirement day, back when he was in Iraq commanding a logistics company and he had a future to look forward to. But now instead of a steak with champagne he reached for a can opener and a Coke. There was no booze in the trailer, a lesson he'd learned well (if a little late).

He found himself humming the song always sung at the end of every retirement ceremony: "Old soldiers never die, never die, never die. Old soldiers never die, they just fade away."

The beans were warmed, the Coke was on ice, and the ketchup flowed freely over Campbell's finest.

He was fading, alright. At the rate he was going, by the end of next month he'd be transparent.

Two

Two weeks later, Ben took his car in for an oil change. With no job prospects, he figured the old heap would have to serve him for a while yet, so best get it taken care of before he got his last share of a full paycheck. He was sitting on a couch in the waiting area, maxing out on free coffee, when he heard shouting in the back. He looked up just in time to see a skinny young man with long sideburns and tattoos up both arms go storming out the back door.

"And don't come back!" the manager yelled just before the door slammed. "Musicians," he muttered, then turned and saw Ben staring at him and froze. "Sorry, sir. Just a little employee counseling."

"Looked like a little employee canceling to me," said Ben. "I understand. In the Army, I had to counsel my soldiers and civilians. Don't think your 'counseling' is going to do him much good."

The manager's white shirt had the name Jerry emblazoned over the right breast pocket that had held the handkerchief he now used to mop his face.

"True enough," he admitted. "He was a pain to work with; still, he was one of the best parts clerks I've ever had. He knew how to manage the inventory and track expenses like no one else. He'll be difficult to replace."

Ben reached into his right breast pocket and pulled out one of the half-dozen or so cards he had left and presented it with more bravado than he felt. "Maybe I can help you."

Jerry looked at the card, then the man in the nice suit who'd handed it to him. "I don't think I can pay you what you're expecting. The job's basically a clerk that runs their own section."

Ben looked the manager in the eye. "I have two more weeks of active duty pay, then I'll either be working at a job somewhere or I'll be eating cat food. I'm divorced with a kid, so the little that will be left over from my pension won't be enough to cover my gas and the rent on my doublewide, so about now all I'm expecting is a living wage. If JP Morgan calls me up and offers me a corner office, I'll give you two weeks notice, but right now your parts manager job sounds pretty good."

"You don't sugarcoat it, Mister ..."

"Fuller, but please, just call me Ben."

"OK, Ben. But before we go back to my office, how soon could you start? I can't go more than a day without someone back there managing the inventory."

"That depends."

"On what?"

"On how soon my car is ready so I can go home and change."

Three

The next day, Ben was in the back of the shop studying the computer system, his name freshly emblazoned over the right pocket of his new blue lab coat. The pay wasn't much—Jerry hadn't lied—but combined with his sliver of a pension it would pay the bills ... just. While plenty of peanut butter sandwiches loomed in his immediate future, it beat cat food.

The day his retirement took effect was just like any other. Ben got up, showered, then went to the sink to shave. Except this time, he found he was out of fresh razor blades. He looked at this reflection in the mirror. He'd already decided to cut back on haircuts.

"Why bother?" he decided and tossed his razor in the trash. "One less thing to worry about."

After three months, he had a nice, thick salt-and-pepper beard. Perhaps he might even try his luck and sneak onto the sidelines at Danny's next game. Yeah, why not? The local paper showed all the schedules for the kids' leagues, and Danny's team was doing well with a good chance of making the playoffs.

That weekend, Ben parked well away from everyone else so Danny wouldn't see his car and brought along a folding chair he set under some trees away from the bleachers. He sipped some tea from his thermos and gradually relaxed as people walked past without giving him a second look. Finally, the teams formed up for pre-game drills, and Danny looked over in his direction. Ben tensed ... Then his son turned back to the exercises with the rest of the team and didn't gaze his way again.

Score one for the home team.

After that, Ben didn't miss a game and was even there at the first elimination game when Danny scored the winning goal. Not running onto the field was one of the hardest things he'd ever done … well, *not* done. Another was a week later when they lost. Watching Danny trudge off the field, his head down, made Ben wince at the distance between them. So near, yet out of reach. Perhaps forever now.

That evening, he looked at the picture of him holding Danny when he was three. They were laughing, at what he couldn't recall. It really didn't matter. They were there together, really together, and he was a hero to his son.

It was a lie, he decided—absence. It doesn't make the heart grow fonder. At least when caused by a series of broken promises.

He looked at the picture of his sister, Susan, in her cap and gown from graduation from Gallaudet College. She was holding her degree in English in one hand and signing "I Love you" with the other. As the big brother to a deaf sister (their dad long gone), he'd protected her all through their childhood. When he watched her walk across the stage and receive her degree, he realized she didn't need him anymore and it was only then he allowed himself to start dating.

How long had it been since he'd seen her?

If you have to stop and count, it's been too long, whatever the number, he thought, not knowing when he could afford the trip.

Summer turned to fall, and as Thanksgiving drew near, one of the mechanics, an amiable fellow named Charley, sat down beside Ben at in the break room as he was trying to remember how old the bread was on his sandwich.

"How's it going, Santa?" he asked.

Ben shrugged. "Not feeling too jolly. It's gonna be a tight Christmas. Why'd you call me Santa, anyway?"

"Well, your beard for one, and civilian life seems to agree with you. I guess since you ain't taking a physical fitness test you've cut back on the sit-ups?"

Ben was on the last notch of his belt, a fact he didn't need Charley to point out.

"So, I look like Santa now? Thanks."

"Hey man, don't get mad. You know what? My brother is the store manager at Hurley's Department Store. He asked me last night if I knew anyone who could fill in for their regular guy. He just got a better offer in Austin, so he bailed a week before Santa Land opens up in the store. He's pretty desperate 'cause their Santa has always had a real beard and he doesn't want to just stick someone there with a fake one unless he absolutely has to. You interested?"

"I dunno. What's it pay?"

"You'd have to ask him, but he's hard up. Reckon you could negotiate a pretty good deal. And shit, he can afford it!"

Ben stroked his beard, a habit he'd begun to pick up. He was tempted. Yeah, he could certainly use the extra income, even if the job would only be until Christmas.

"Sounds good, but what about my job here? Jerry wouldn't hold my job for six weeks. I wouldn't if I were him."

"Pretty sure it's nights and weekends." Charley pulled a card out of his pocket and wrote his name on the back. "Here's my brother's card. Tell him I sent you, and he'll at least hear you out. What have you got to lose? Apart from your dignity!" He guffawed and slapped Ben on the back playfully.

Ben looked down at his bologna and cheese sandwich, then took the card.

Four

Charley's brother was named Mike, and Mike lit up like one of his store's fake Christmas trees when Ben showed up at his door.

"I think I'm in love! Where you been all my life?"

"Excuse me?" Ben said. "I heard you were looking for a Santa."

"Am I ever! If I don't get the right man by tomorrow, I may have to get a fake beard and do it myself. Hurley's has been around for seventy years, and a lot of families have a tradition of getting their picture with our Santa every year. For seventy years he's had a real beard, and I'd hate to be the manager who broke that record!"

"I have no experience."

"You'll get it."

"My beard's not all white."

"We can color it."

"I work with your brother, Charley. I can only work after-hours and weekends."

"That's just when we'll need you."

"I don't know how much the job pays."

"I'll make it worth your while, with a nice bonus if you stay the whole season."

"I'm not a very jolly old elf."

Mike's smile faded for a moment. "Look, I'm not asking you to promise these kids anything except that you'll do your best. Your job is to listen and let them know they've been heard." He sighed. "That's really all most people want ... Christ, if I'd figured that out ten years ago I'd still be married to my first wife."

The extra pay would be nice—maybe he could take a trip to California next year. And it was a pleasant change to have someone *want* to hire him. Maybe he could give the bologna a rest once in a while and

43

splurge on a burger. He looked down at his belt. A veggie burger.

"When do I start?"

"You're on the payroll as of today, though you'll have to pass a background check before I can let you be with children. Anything I should know, Ben?"

He swallowed. "Yeah ... um, one thing, Mike. I've had a DUI."

Mike's smile faded. "How many times?"

"Just once, eighteen months ago. I haven't touched a drop since, I swear."

"Honestly, Ben, if I had any other options right now, I'd turn you down, but if everything else checks out, the job's still yours if you want it." He pointed his index finger right between Ben's eyes like a pistol. "But if I ever get a single whiff of alcohol on you on the job, you'll be in the parking lot before you can say 'cookies.' Got it?"

"Yes, Mike. I got it, and I don't blame you. Thanks for the chance. I won't let you down."

Mike's smile returned with just a slight edge. "I'll take you to HR and we'll fill out the paperwork, then our seamstress will fit you for the costume. Santa makes his big arrival the day after Thanksgiving, so one week from tomorrow."

"OK, Mike, you've got yourself a Santa. Let's do it."

"Great!" Mike rose to guide Ben to HR, when he paused. "One last thing. Let me hear your 'ho'!"

"My what?"

"Your 'ho.' You know, as in 'Ho, ho, ho!'"

Ben took a deep breath and bellowed his best "Ho, ho, ho!"

Mike shook his head. "Work on that. It came from your throat. Santa has belly laughs. You need to belt it out from deep inside you. You look the part, and you look fit enough to lift small children all night, but you gotta have the laugh. Trust me, the kids will spot you as a fake in a heartbeat if you ain't got the 'ho.'"

"I'll ... work on it."

"OK, Santa Ben. Let's get you hired!"

Five

The next day at work, Ben noticed Jerry had decorated the waiting room with Christmas lights and carols were playing on the loudspeaker. Ben was opening up the door to the parts department when Jerry came by with a sprig of mistletoe pinned over his name.

"Hey, Santa! Charley told me you'll be moonlighting at Hurley's!"

Ben's head started to hurt. "It's part-time. Don't worry, I won't let it interfere with my work here."

Jerry frowned. "Easy there, bud. I wasn't busting your chops. I think it's great! This being your first year you wouldn't know this, but we do a food giveaway the Saturday before Christmas. I usually wear a fake beard and hand out the baskets, but this year ... well, let's just say you're hired ... again!"

Ben gave a weak grin, mostly hidden by his beard. "Sure, boss. Whatever you say."

Jerry paused. "It's not part of the job, Ben. Seriously, don't do it if you don't want to, but if your job at Hurley's doesn't interfere and you'd like to do it, I've got the costume I always wear. Let me know next week. If you say yes, I can bring in my suit to see how it fits. Don't decide now, you look like you've got a lot on your mind. I'll check in with you next week."

Jerry went off, humming a Christmas carol while Ben returned to the sanctuary of the parts department. Keeping an inventory was almost a religion to him. He had no idea what most of the parts did but could tell you how many widgets of each kind he had and exactly where they rested until needed. He wished his life had the same kind of order and certainty.

Once he got home from work, he called Emily. He knew his name would pop up in her caller ID and was prepared to leave a message when she answered.

"Hello, Ben."

Ben noticed there was no "How are you?" or "How's it going?" Just an acknowledgment the call was from him. *Well, at least she picked up.*

"Hello, Emily. I was wondering how things are going with Danny. I've got a part-time job for the holidays and would like to get him something nice for Christmas. Any ideas?"

"All the years we lived together you always left it to me to buy his presents, and now that we're divorced you still want me to pick them out for you? If you spent some time with him—"

"If he *let* me spend some time with him, maybe I wouldn't have to ask!"

Emily sighed. "OK, maybe I can drive up to your trailer and open the door, but I'm not gonna drag him out of the car. You'll have to do that."

Ben took a deep breath. "Let's start again. I want to get our son a Christmas present, something he'd like. I'm not asking you to buy it. I just need an idea or two."

"Give him some money. He'll buy what he wants."

"That's not the same thing! It's like bribing him to love me."

There was a long pause, and Ben thought Emily had hung up when she spoke again, a slight catch to her voice. "I think it's too late for that, Ben. I've tried to talk to him about seeing you, but he clams up ..." There was another pause. "Ben, I've ... I've started seeing someone. He works here—in another office. He's divorced with a son about Danny's age. We've gone out a couple of times, the four of us, and Danny seems to like him and his son a lot."

"What! Just like that?! We've only been divorced six months!"

"A year, Ben. Almost. Do the math. We got divorced in February."

"Yeah, now I remember. Groundhog Day. At least it wasn't Valentine's Day."

"I'm hanging up now, Ben."

"Wait! Once I get Danny something, can I at least bring it over?"

"OK. But don't just show up. I need to get Danny ready for you."

"Yeah, and your boyfriend out of the house. I get it."

"Don't press your luck, Ben. Call me when you want to bring something to the house. Goodbye."

His phone went dead, and Ben dropped it before he flung it across the room. He didn't have the money for a new one.

Merry Christmas, he thought.

Six

It was the night of Santa's arrival at Hurley's, and Ben's mouth was as dry as a desert, though his armpits were soaked beneath the fur of the red coat. San Antonio, Texas, rarely merited more than a thick sweater in winter, and tonight the low was in the fifties. Ben was already dreading the heat of the photographer's lights.

Too late now.

Mike had arranged for the local fire department to drive him up to the store with their lights flashing and the siren wailing, as was part of the Hurley's tradition. Santa always made a grand entrance, and this year would be no exception.

The fire captain looked him over as he helped buckle Ben in at the rendezvous site a mile away. "You're new. What happened to the old guy?"

"He got a better offer in Austin, I heard."

The fireman shook his head. "I can't imagine a better job than being Santa at Hurley's. People will love you. I mean it, love you. This is my twentieth run, and it's the happiest thing I do all year." He patted Ben on the shoulder once he was belted in. "You're the luckiest man I know."

Ben swallowed when he saw the crowd. *Jeez, must be five-hundred!*

Half were parents and half were children, grouped together at the store's entrance to greet him. He could hear them cheering as soon as the siren died. The firemen made a big production of helping him out of the fire truck and down the tall steps. Mike was standing in front of the crowd with a microphone shouting out, "And here he is, SANTA CLAUS!! Say hello to the people here, Santa!"

Ben had memorized his lines and walked to the microphone with the same enthusiasm he'd had when he climbed the steps for his retirement ceremony. *So, this is how it ends*, he mused. *A fat man in a red suit, selling junk to children.*

"Merry Christmas and welcome to Hurley's!" he shouted with all the enthusiasm he could muster. Luckily, the roar of the crowd largely drowned him out. Most of them were regulars.

Hell, they probably know the script better than me!

Mike bowed slightly, swept his arm toward the entrance, and proclaimed, "Make way! Time for Santa to lead us in!"

This is it … Ben took a deep breath and using his chest as a bellows forced out his "Ho, ho, ho!"

He'd been practicing all week in the car to and from work, getting odd looks once from an old lady who'd stopped beside him at a red light. He was definitely louder than his first effort back in Mike's office, and it seemed to pass muster as the crowd surged toward the entrance, some children bouncing along beside their parents.

Ben swung his arms like a toy soldier on parade to give himself a joyful swagger, and soon several of the children were marching alongside, their small bodies swaying in time to his. *It's really working!* Ben thought and was caught off guard by his own laugh.

The throne was a high-backed chair lined in red velvet and with gold paint on the arms and trim all the way down the legs, perched on a small platform perhaps two feet off the floor with enough space around him for families to gather and grin at the camera.

Two of the employees' teenage daughters were his elves, fitted in green tights, red jackets, and, Ben presumed, fake ears. They were responsible for line management and helping children up and down the platform or into Santa's lap. When Ben arrived at Santa Land, their eyes widened at the sight of the merry mob headed toward them.

Time to rally the troops. "Ho, ho, ho!" he said, without even thinking about it, smiling at his two cowed helpers. "Hello, my friends, time to make some Christmas Magic!"

Then he lowered his chin and speaking in a voice just loud enough for them to hear, added, "Don't worry. We've got this." They looked at each other, then him, and smiled.

"The line forms here to see Santa!" the one with "Mistletoe" on her nametag said, and just like that, an orderly line of noisy and excited children, parents in tow, formed exactly where it was supposed to.

Ben quickly learned that babies were the easiest. They couldn't ask for anything, weren't afraid of him (yet), and always looked adorable, at least to the parents and/or grandparents paying the photographer. It seemed there were no bad baby pictures.

Children three to five were the hardest, often needing bribery to hold still or even approach him. Ben tried to remember what it had been like when Danny was that age and they took him to see Santa, but he couldn't. Then he realized why. Emily always had to take him herself.

One boy around ten, Danny's age, held back until finally, prodded by his mother he stepped forward.

"What would you like for Christmas?" Ben asked, the words now flowing.

"It's OK, sir." The boy said, refusing to sit on his lap. "I know you're pretend. I'm just here to make my mom happy." He looked up at Ben. "The one thing I want most is the one thing you can't give me." He sighed. "Let's just do the picture."

Ben put his hand on the boy's shoulder and turned him slowly toward the camera. The boy didn't smile but lifted his chin and looked straight ahead. The cameraman always took three shots, and for some reason Ben took his hand off the boy's shoulder for the third one and put it behind his head, two fingers up in the classic "bunny ears" pose.

He heard a gasp in the line and saw the woman who'd brought him with one tear running down her cheek. She went forward to the boy he assumed was her son, and when they reviewed the third shot, they embraced. They turned to go, but the mother hesitated, looked back at him, and mouthed, "Thank you."

Ben nodded, puzzled, relieved she wasn't angry, and promptly forgot about it.

When Santa Land had closed for the night, he turned to his elves, saw the light in their eyes, and knew they were now veterans. Tomorrow they'd be ready for anything. He turned to go to the back, to change, when each young woman said, "Good night, Santa."

It sounded pretty good.

He was also now an expert on the Christmas wishes of a healthy sample of boys Danny's age. A very good night indeed.

When he got to his locker, he saw a sticky note saying, "See me before you go," signed Mike.

Here it comes, Ben thought, *a Performance Review after my first night.* He rubbed the back of his neck, changed into his secret identity of Ben Fuller, mild-mannered auto-parts clerk, and trudged up the stairs to see if he would have to surrender his throne.

Mike was on the phone, his back to the door when Ben came to the entrance. He hesitated. *Might as well get this over with*, and he rapped his knuckles softly on the doorframe. Mike looked over his shoulder, motioned for Ben to take a seat, and finished the call. "Look, Marge, I gotta go. My Santa's just come up to see me. I'll be home in an hour. Love you!"

Ben liked the sound of "my" Santa. He hoped it was still true.

Mike spun around in his swivel chair and smiled. "Nice first day, Ben. Really. I like how you got the girls calmed down, too. After five minutes, it was like the three of you'd been working together for years."

"Thanks, Mike," Ben said, still uneasy calling his boss by his first name. "Was there anything in particular you wanted to see me about?"

"I know you're tired. I just wanted to say you had a great first night, and I wanted to ask you about one family I saw, crying and hugging as they left. What did you say to them?"

"I'm sorry if I upset them. The boy seemed real sad, so I gave him bunny ears on the last shot. I don't know, it was just an impulse. His mom teared up when she saw me do it, then he did when he saw the shot. That's all I know."

Mike shrugged. "Let's just call it some Christmas Magic, then. Seems like it was the right thing to do, for whatever reason. Anyway, was a good night." He looked up at the entrance to his office. "Ah, it seems I've got a date with an elf."

There in a hooded sweatshirt and torn jeans, minus her enlarged ears, was Mistletoe. "Hi, Dad," she said. "Ready to go? I'm going to Angela's house for a sleepover and I'm already late."

"Sure thing, your Elfness! Let's go home. See you tomorrow, Ben. And thanks again."

On the way home, Ben noticed the "check engine" light came on. He gripped the steering wheel a little tighter. *Christ, I don't have time for this.* He sighed. He didn't have the money for it, either.

He kept driving, sniffing for smoke all the while, but he made it back to the trailer park without the car stalling out. This time.

He sagged as he crossed the threshold into his trailer. The physical work wasn't demanding, but the tightrope of emotions he'd walked since leaving the fire truck left him stumbling toward his bed as he tugged his clothes off, casually throwing them on a chair before sliding beneath the blanket, the glow of his small space heater the only light in his sleeping cubicle.

Seven

It was around two in the morning when he woke, feeling the presence of someone else in the darkness, standing over him. His eyes blurry, he looked up. A woman. He blinked and squinted. A small woman who smelled of ... cookies?

"Hello, Ben. It's been a long time."

By the glow of the purring heater, he saw a woman less than five feet tall, dressed in a flouncy skirt, fur-trimmed cape, and white fur hat, looking at him with a frown as though to say he wasn't at all what she'd expected. Something about her eyes made him feel they'd met before ... If only he could remember where and when.

"What? Do I know you, lady, and what are you doing in my trailer? How did you even get in?"

"Oh, please! Doors and locks don't affect us."

"Us? You belong to a burglar guild?"

"Don't be silly, Ben. Burglars take things, we leave them."

"How do you know my name? What is all this?" He stopped. "Ah. I'm dreaming, right?"

His lady visitor sighed and handed him a newspaper from somewhere beneath her cape. "Last week you read an article that people can't understand print in dreams, remember that? Well, here's a copy of tomorrow's San Antonio Gazette. Maybe that'll convince you."

Ben took the paper and looked down to see the San Antonio Spurs would lose to Denver the following night, 88 to 102. *Very* unlikely. Denver hadn't beat the Spurs once the past two seasons.

"OK, I can read, though this is obviously fake. Now what?"

She put her hands on her hips and scowled. In the faint light, she looked like an angry doll.

"It's about Danny. His light is going out, but I think after what you did tonight at Hurley's that maybe, with our help, you can still save him."

"What?! Is he in the hospital ...? Is he ..." He rubbed his eyes, trying to shake the fog from his mind. "Wait ... Are you threatening me? Have you done anything to him?"

She clucked her tongue. "We've done nothing to him but try to keep his Christmas spirit, Ben. But we're losing him ... Like we lost you."

"Look, lady ..."

"Claus. Mrs. Claus."

"Yes, of course you are. Now it all makes sense. Where's Rudolph?"

Ben stood up and reached for his pants. "I'm only getting dressed because I want my clothes on when the police arrive. It's up to you if you're still here when ..."

He'd no sooner zipped up his trousers when he found himself in a large room filled with small people with headphones over their pointed ears, scanning video monitors.

The sudden change had his head spinning, and for a moment he thought he was going to throw up.

"What the hel—"

"Language, Ben, please!" Mrs. Claus tilted her head toward the little people at their stations before helping him into a chair he would have sworn wasn't there a moment ago.

Ben looked around, wordless for the moment as he tried to grasp what had just happened. He shivered. His small abductor lifted her left hand and a small ...

well, *elf*, for lack of a better term, came up to her from a coffee pot in the corner.

"Yes, Mrs. C?"

"Our guest here, Ben, needs some slippers and a robe."

"Of course, ma'am." He turned to go, then looked back at Ben and handed him his mug. "This should hold you till I get back."

Ben sniffed the mug, grateful for the warmth in his hands. If a bit unhappy about the small size of the mug. He sniffed it ... Mmm, cocoa. Its rich, tempting aroma engulfed him. He meant to sip it, but it was so warm and rich he drained it in one go and his stomach returned to its happy place.

He looked around. "I guess you're gonna tell me I'm at the North Pole and these little guys, uh, and girls," he amended as a small young lady walked by, "are ... elves?"

"Yes, Ben. And I'm Mrs. Claus and you're at the North Pole. Well, more under it, actually." She pointed up. "Satellites, you know."

"Of course. Satellites."

A large red, fleece-lined robe approached him, with two small feet beneath it. Ben picked it up, finding the cocoa elf underneath with a pair of slippers under one arm.

"Here you go, Mister Ben," the elf said, handing over the slippers as Ben stood to wrap the robe around his frozen frame. "I hope they fit. They're the largest size we have."

"Thank you, Wilfred," Mrs. Claus said. "I'll take it from here. You can go back to your monitor, now."

The elf mock saluted and scurried off to a monitor close to the cocoa dispenser and put his headset back on.

Ben looked around, convinced this was all a dream. *Might as well go with it and have a good time*, he decided. He looked at the tiny mug in his hand. *Cocoa this good could never exist in real life.* "OK, I'll bite. Why am I here?"

Mrs. Claus peered deeply into his eyes. "You still don't believe me, do you?"

"What does it matter what I believe?"

"Because, Ben, without belief, we couldn't do what we do. We'd ..." she looked around the large room of elves, "disappear forever."

"Maybe if I knew what you do, I'd find it easier to believe. Where is the toyshop, for example? Aren't your elves supposed to be hammering out dolls and toy soldiers?"

The corners of her mouth made a small, half-smile. "Long ago, when there weren't billions of people, yes, we made toys, knitted sweaters, and cooked Christmas pies to leave in the homes of those who believed in and welcomed us. Now, though, there are just too many of you! Oh, we still make some gifts for those who need them the most, of course. But for the most part, we give something more valuable, and transportable."

"You mean gift cards?" Ben asked. "That's what I give when I don't know what else to do. And you don't have to gift wrap them, either."

"No!" She stamped her foot. "This is serious, Ben. We give something more important. We give people Christmas spirit, and we do it all through the year, not just on Christmas Day. If we waited until then, it would be too late."

"What's this got to do with Danny? You said his 'light' was going out. What's that mean?"

"I think it best if I show you what we do, then how you helped someone tonight."

She took him by the hand and led him to the nearest elf in front of a monitor.

"Who are you monitoring right now, Linnea?"

"Jack Duncan, twelve years old."

"A difficult age, twelve. Does he still believe?"

"Not exactly, Mrs. C. But he still loves Christmas."

"Good! What have you done for him today?"

"Well, I reminded him of the bike he got when he was six, then I got him to mention it to his dad. They're going on a bike ride after his dad gets home from work."

"Excellent work, Linnea!" She pulled a clipboard off a hook beside the monitor. "I see by your worksheet that he worries about a bully at school, so maybe this will give him a chance to tell his father and have the two of them work on it together."

Linnea smiled at Mrs. C's praise. "That's my goal for the week, to get them into one serious talk about growing up. That's gotten a lot harder since smartphones came out."

The little woman sighed and patted the elf on the shoulder. "I know, dear. Nowadays people mostly talk *at* other people while they stare at a small screen, not *with* them. If they even talk at all. It's all 'emojis.' Well, keep up the good work and let me know how the bike ride goes."

She turned to Ben. "Mostly, we whisper into people's ears. Make them pause when a favorite Christmas song comes on the radio. Push a favorite toy from their childhood back into their memory and give them a touch of the magic they believed in before they got too old." She looked at Ben. "And cynical. There is a wisdom in innocence. It isn't cool to believe in goodness anymore, or to trust someone enough to drop your armor. The world is getting colder and children too old, too soon."

She led Ben to a larger monitor in the middle of the room. "Now I want to show you why I brought you here." She pointed to the chair in front. "Please sit. This won't take long." She turned to a microphone beside the monitor. "Chad, please report to central station."

A young male elf popped into view at Ben's left elbow almost immediately. He looked at Ben and started. "It's you! The Santa from Hurley's. Wow, great job, dude! You brought little Freddy back to us." He held his hand up for a high-five, which Ben tapped out, not wanting to hurt the little guy.

Mrs. C nodded toward the monitor. "Ben doesn't yet understand what he did. Can you show him?"

"Sure thing!" The little man turned to the controls, and soon Ben saw himself from the perspective of someone much shorter than himself, which he assumed must be Freddy's point of view.

He reviewed the tape and was surprised to hear his own voice through the ears of a child. He sounded too loud, brassy even. No wonder some children were afraid of him.

The pictures were taken quickly, and Freddy was standing with his mother looking at the monitor to choose which images, if any, they'd have printed. When the third one flashed up on the screen, Freddy froze.

"Just like Grandpa," his mother said. "Santa couldn't bring him back, but maybe this was his way of saying your grandfather still loves you even if you can't see him anymore, just like you still love him."

Freddy and his mother hugged, and the clip stopped there.

Ben sat still, a small tear in the corner of his eye he refused to wipe away. "I didn't know. I was just clowning around. It doesn't mean anything."

Chad cleared his throat. "Doesn't mean anything? You gave that boy hope and restored his Christmas spirit." He shook his head. "That's all we live for up here. You did in an instant what I couldn't do in the three months since his grandfather died. Man, that's *every*thing to us."

Ben shrugged. "Beginner's luck." He looked up at Mrs. C. "OK, thanks for the show. I'll try to do it again tomorrow, but I need to get back home now."

Mrs. Claus's eyes were level with his as he sat, and she leaned in close as she said, "I have a favor to ask before I send you back."

Ben stood up and pushed the seat back. "Anything to go home. I want to wake up in my bed and find you and all this ..." he waved at the room, "gone and filed away as a dream."

"Very well, Ben. Here's our situation: I need you to help me rescue Danny's Christmas spirit. His candle has gone out, and if we don't act soon, he'll be empty and unhappy the rest of his life."

"But how can I help? He won't even come see me!"

"Can you blame him? You were always too busy trying to win the next promotion."

"That's what fathers do! They provide for their families," Ben insisted.

"Where did you learn that?"

"When I was twelve, and if you're who you say you are, you'll know why."

Mrs. Claus paused, then took Ben's right hand in both of hers. "Yes, I do. And you had to provide for your mother and sister since the day your father left. But fathers also give themselves. You never made time for that."

Ben jerked his hand back and turned away, looking for an exit. "I wouldn't know. I thought making sure your family didn't go hungry was pretty important."

He turned to glare down at the small woman. "It's not like I had an example to go by."

"You did, Ben. You just learned the wrong lessons from them."

I what ...? Ben scratched his head. This *felt* real. He couldn't remember ever being cold in a dream before, or tasting hot cocoa, and like the little woman said, he was able to read and understand print. But Santa? Elves? Now Danny's "candle"? This was too much.

"OK, lady. I don't know what you slipped into that cocoa or how you got into my trailer, or even where we really are, but it's time for me to wake up in my own bed and get ready for work. Now be a nice witch, will you, and click your heels together three times, or whatever you have to do, and send me back. I'm done."

Mrs. Claus frowned, then turned to the microphone again. "Philip to the central monitor, please."

Ben blinked, and there beside Mrs. C. was an older, bearded elf dressed in a dapper gray wool suit and a red brocade vest. He bowed, and in a proper British accent said, "Yes, madam, I've been expecting your summons." He looked at Ben with a face you get when you step in something unpleasant. "This will be Danny in his room with the son of his mother's new boyfriend." He turned to the monitor and quickly brought up the video. Danny was sitting on his bed, talking to a blond-haired boy his age sitting across the room from him.

"Do you ever see your dad?" the other boy asked.

"No. He never had time for me when we lived together. Now he just wants to see me to get back at Mom." He looked out the window. "Don't think I was important to him before, and I haven't changed, so why would he? No matter how hard I tried to get good grades, make the soccer team, clean my room, he was too busy. I gave up. It hurts less that way." Danny turned back to the other boy. "Your dad is cool. Likes spending time with you, and us. I hope … I hope he and my mom get married."

The video stopped there. Philip sat still, waiting for Ben to say something.

Ben looked down and saw his hands were shaking and stuffed them into his pockets, hoping no one had seen. "Boys talk like that sometimes," he said, his voice unsteady.

Philip turned back to the monitor. "I have some other clips I could—"

"No! I mean, no, thank you. That's enough." Ben sighed from deep inside, the same way Mike had wanted him to laugh. "I get your point." He turned to Mrs. Claus. "What can I do? What can *we* do? Can you help me get my son back?"

She cocked her head to one side. "What do you mean get him back? You've lost him. He will never want to live with you if that's what you want. But …" She paused.

"Yeah? But what?"

"Maybe we can still save his Christmas spirit. No, I don't mean make him believe in us—that's not necessary to be happy. But the Christmas spirit isn't just for six weeks of the year. We try to refresh people's joy in life, to see the beauty all around them, and then do our best to keep it strong throughout the year."

"So, what the Christmas spirit is like a … like a 'booster shot' of happiness to help people get through the coming year?"

Mrs. Claus laughed, the sound like water trickling in a brook. "Yes, exactly like that!"

"Huh. So how do we do this? Give Danny his booster shot." He looked at her and Philip. "You two seem to know him better than I do."

Philip cleared his throat. "First, we'll have to get him to agree to see you."

"Right," Ben sighed. "Like the recipe for duck soup. First, get a duck. I understand that part. How can I get him to agree to see me?"

Mrs. C pulled a calendar out from beneath her robe. "The only time you can see him between now and Christmas is in the mornings on weekends. I've found that two things divorced dads can do with their children on short notice is go to the movies or ..."

"The zoo? Yeah, the guys I know who got divorced all seem to end up at the zoo with their kids. It's almost a rite of passage." Ben shook his head. "It's weird, but somehow taking Danny to the zoo is like saying I'll never be his full-time father again."

Philip clicked his tongue. "Movies it is then. He did mention something to the other boy, who's named Steve, by the way." Philip wrote down something on a piece of paper and handed it to Ben.

Ben squinted at the name. "He's too young for this. Besides, this isn't animated. He only likes Disney movies."

Mrs. C looked over her glasses. "He did when you last took him at age seven. He's growing, Ben. That's what happens when you feed them regularly. Now he likes explosions and car chases, and because that's what the other boys like."

"If Emily even lets me take him, how can I get him to agree?"

"How did you get Emily to go out with you?"

"I asked her."

"So, start with that. Maybe invite Steve along? But if you do, don't call him Stevie—he so hates that!"

"You want me to ask my rival's son along? You're crazy!"

"The boy is Danny's friend. Do you want him to have a good time or 'perform his duty' as your son? And Emily. Might she be more likely to agree if you take the other boy along, do you think?"

"No! Absolutely not. I'm not paying for another man's kid to spy on me for the little time I'd have with Danny. Any other bright ideas?"

Philip and Mrs. C exchanged a look, then she shrugged. "OK, Ben. We'll try it your way. It's time to send you home." She walked over and took his hand. "Now, close your eyes, I don't want you to get dizzy."

Her hand faded away ...

And Ben found himself back in the trailer in bed. Of course, he was in bed!

But in bed with his trousers on?

He sat up and rubbed his eyes. "Hello? Mrs. Claus?"

He looked around. *Alone.* He got out of bed to take his pants off, then hunkered back down.

"Crazy dream," he mumbled before dropping into a deep sleep. His last thought of the night was that the trailer had the odd scent of freshly baked cookies.

Eight

The next day being Saturday, Ben was free until 1 p.m. Santa Land opened at 2 p.m. and ran until 8 p.m., so Mike wanted him there an hour beforehand to prepare and have a leisurely lunch as he wouldn't eat again until after the store closed.

Ben had asked Mike for an advance on his pay for Christmas shopping, but the store manager made him a counteroffer.

"I can't give you an advance, Ben, sorry. It's against store policy. But I tell you what, how about I give you an employee discount of twenty percent and take the purchase out of your paycheck. How's that?"

Not having much choice, Ben agreed, so he was soon on his way to his first shopping expedition as a single dad. The store was three stories high with a fully stocked basement. Santa Land was on the ground floor to give it the easiest access, but the toys were in the basement and that's where he headed. As he looked at the prices for the newest electronic gadgets most boys seemed to want, he swallowed. Even with his discount, a drone would cost him about sixteen hours in the chair. A video game that had just come out was pretty popular, but Ben had no way of knowing if Danny already had it.

Then there was the fear that no matter what he got for Danny, Emily's new boyfriend would go one better. No, he probably couldn't beat his rival on price. He'd have to use his knowledge of Danny to get him something most other boys wouldn't ask for.

Then it came to him, and he took the escalator up to the top floor, to the Children's Clothing Department. As he stowed his purchase into a small bag, he checked his watch. Noon. Might as well eat here at the cafeteria. He'd eaten there a couple of times before and he'd grown fond of their meatloaf. Ben could fry an egg and make pancakes, but his cooking skills never got much beyond that. He'd be happy to discover the joy so many women had known for generations: eating a meal they'd neither prepared nor would have to clean up after.

He was chewing slowly, enjoying the simple pleasure of a simple meal, when a red-haired woman came by with her tray. She motioned to the empty seat across from his, and Ben nodded. "Please, join me."

She sat down and introduced herself as Moira Kincaid. Ben was immediately taken with her soft Irish accent and teasing green eyes that seemed to hint at some secret only she knew. "I'm the manager in Housewares, next to Santa Land. I saw you last weekend, by the way. You made a grand entrance, you did."

"Ben Kincaid is my secret identity," he said, putting a finger to his lips as though cautioning her to keep it to herself while loving the way she said "Grand." He smiled suddenly. No one had ever described his entrance as "grand" before.

"Something funny?" she said, her eyebrows raised. "You think my accent is funny?"

"Not at all, Moira," Ben said. "I think it's 'grand,'" doing his best to imitate her voice, and they both laughed.

"You're a cheeky Father Christmas, I must say. Not at all like the other lad. He only smiled when he was on the clock."

Ben shrugged. "His loss," all the while thinking the meatloaf had never tasted so good.

"So how did a fair Irish lass wind up in Texas?"

She snorted, "Careful, Ben. Best leave the Blarney to the Irish, we're better at it."

She took a bite out of her lasagna before answering. "I was married to a man who got work here in America. The marriage didn't last, and I'd made friends here so it was just easier to stay, though I usually go back to Ireland for Christmas. I'll be flying back two days before and stay until January the fourth. No one does Christmas better than the Irish. If you ever forsake the cloth, I mean robe, you should find out for yourself."

Ben wiped his beard to reduce the meatloaf stain. He'd still have to wash and dye it before going on the throne but best not to let the tomato sauce set too long. That's when Moira noticed his wedding ring.

"Ah, sorry. I didn't know you were married. The way you talked, I ..."

"Oh, I'm divorced. Almost ten months now. I haven't taken the ring off yet because, well, that would mean there was no hope ..."

"Of getting her back? Aye, I know. It was easier for me—I left him and good riddance. He was a bastard at times, but the funny thing is, I still miss him off and on, though mostly off. I miss him when I'm driving alone, eating alone, talking to myself, and sleeping alone. I don't mean just the ... well, you know, the physical, but just someone to warm me on a cold night." She laughed. "I considered a cat, but that'd be my sign of surrender, wouldn't it?"

"Ah, yes. And you know what they say about crazy cat ladies. That might be a sign of desperation, alright."

She froze, and Ben feared he'd strayed too close, too soon. She looked down at her plate. "Aye, a dog then." She stood and picked up her tray. "Well, Ben, nice meeting you. I've something to do. I'll see you on the throne," and she left without a look back.

Idiot, Ben! He sighed and returned to his meatloaf, noting it now tasted pretty much as it always did.

It was a busy night in Santa Land, and Ben only had a couple of pauses in the line when he could look off to his right at Housewares. He thought he glimpsed Moira once, helping a customer, but a terrified three-year-old boy was being herded in his direction and Ben had to do his best to soothe the child for his big moment. Once the pictures were done, he looked again, but she was gone.

He still doubted that the visit the night before was anything other than a lucid dream, one where you know you're dreaming as it happens, but he still softened his voice and noticed the children were less reluctant to come to him, so there was that.

After the store closed, he saw Moira heading out the door and they exchanged cautious smiles, but before he could say anything more, she was gone into the night and he went to his old car, alone. There were few things in his life he could depend on at the moment, but the "check engine" light was as faithful as it had been since it first came on. He couldn't deal with the suspense of waiting for the engine to blow up much longer. Monday, he'd have it looked at and see what sort of bill he was facing and how long he could put it off.

He was listening to the radio when the sports news came on and the announcer gave the scores for the games that night.

San Antonio had lost to Denver, 88 to 102.

Huh ...?

Nine

The next morning Ben called Emily. She answered on the second ring. *Least she didn't have to think about it,* he mused, taking it as a good sign.

"Yes, Ben. What's up?"

"I was wondering if I could take Danny to the movies this Saturday. I have to be at work by one, so it would have to be the morning show."

"What movie were you thinking about?"

"There's that new spy movie I've heard about. It's PG-13, but—"

"He's only ten. Don't you think he's a little young for that?"

"But a lot of the boys I see at work ask to see it."

"Wait. You never said what your part-time job was. Are you working at a movie theater?"

Ben swallowed. "Uh, no. Not a movie theater."

"Then what? What are you not telling me?"

"OK, I'll tell you. Just don't laugh. Please."

"No promises."

Ben swallowed. "I'm the Santa at Hurley's Department Store."

"You're *what?*" There was a long pause, and Ben wasn't sure but he thought he heard suppressed giggling on the other end.

Then, finally, "I … well, I'm impressed. I mean … How's it working out anyway?"

"Better than I expected. The first day was kinda rough, but people want to believe, or at least act like they believe. All I have to do is let them. I've never felt like this before, seeing people smile just to see me. I like it."

"Sounds like it's good for you … and I'm happy for you. Really. So, I guess if I can't trust Santa Claus, who can I? What time's the movie?"

"There's an 8 a.m. show with a pancake breakfast." He paused. "Hey, if Danny wants … maybe your boyfriend's son could come along. Danny might feel more comfortable around me with another kid his own age."

"You'd share the time with Steve? Well, that's … that's good. And I guess I wouldn't have to make breakfast. And Gary and I could have a morning alone, so … Sorry. Sure, I think we have a deal if Danny says yes. Wait a minute and I'll ask him."

"Could I maybe ask him myself?"

"Let's take it one step at a time. Hang on."

He heard Emily call out, and after a brief discussion between mother and son she came back on the phone. "I'm sorry, he said no. Not even with Steve along. I'm sorry, Ben. Really. Maybe we can try again after Christmas? Oh, which reminds me, did you get Danny's present?"

Ben had to put the phone down for a moment, feeling like he'd just been punched in the gut. If he couldn't get his son to come to see a spy movie, with pancakes and his new friend, what would it take? He'd certainly known the gap between them was wide. Now he finally understood how deep it was.

Maybe I've lost him forever. He shook his head. *Not yet. I don't lose him until I quit trying to reach him.* "His present? Yeah, I did. I think I may have chosen a winner, too," he said with more cheerfulness than he felt. "It's too soon to drop it off, though. I'll be working Christmas Eve. Maybe I could come by Christmas morning?" He swallowed bile. "I could, you know, maybe leave it on the front porch or something."

When Emily spoke again, he heard a tone he'd not heard in a very long time. Softer. "Let's see, Ben. How about I work on it from my end? Call me Christmas Day before you come over and I'll tell you if he's ready to see you. OK?"

"Yeah, OK then. We'll talk then. Please tell Danny for me that I love him very much."

"I will, Ben. I know it's true. I'm sorry if my being mad at you made you feel like I ever believed different."

"I just want Danny to know that," Ben said, looking at the gaily wrapped present with Danny's name on it in bold letters while he prayed for a Christmas miracle.

Ten

Between the days at the dealership and the nights and weekends on the throne, the time flew by. He saw Moira a couple of times in the break room, and she nodded with a polite smile when she saw him but didn't ask to sit with him again. Ben wondered what he'd said wrong but was too afraid of the answer to approach her. He'd like to get to know her better, but it seemed this Christmas was fresh out of miracles. He quit ordering the meatloaf.

He'd agreed to do the charity event for the dealership, and Jerry, in return, fixed his car for free. Ben didn't ask what the problem was, but after four hours in the shop the check engine light didn't come on, so he had one less thing to worry about. Maybe that was his Christmas miracle for this year.

On the Saturday morning of the food donation, Jerry drove him in a company tow truck. Not as impressive as a fire truck, but at least the mechanics had cleaned it up and put a big red bow on the hood. Ben already felt like a veteran and threw himself into the role the minute he climbed down, hugging the kids as they mobbed him and giving one "Ho, ho, ho!" after another that made everyone smile. After hours on the throne, he'd found the best medicine for his pain was to make someone else happy.

Better late than never.

The local television station had a reporter and cameraman on the scene, both looking bored, and they quickly faded out of his awareness. He wasn't there for them.

Most of the food had been given out and the cameraman had pulled out his case to put everything away, when Ben saw one little girl about six who had been hanging back from the other children. Thinking she was afraid, he walked slowly up to her. The girl took one look at him and tried to hide behind her mother's long coat but peeked around the edge as he drew near.

Ben squatted down so they were almost eye-to-eye, unaware of the reporter nudging the cameraman to pick his instrument back up, just in case.

"Hello, my friend," Ben said to the face half-hidden behind the coat, when the mother shook her head, a tear in her eyes.

"Jennie's deaf, Santa. I'm sorry. She's too young to know how to lip-read yet. We're just here for the food."

Ben looked up at the mother for a moment, then back to Jennie, and winked. *"Hello, Jennie,"* he signed. *"You're a very pretty girl, and I'm so happy to see you today."*

Jennie's wary face bloomed into pure bliss as she hugged Ben before she began frantically signing her wish list for Christmas. The cameraman had a hard time keeping the proper focus, as Santa and Jennie had a proper Christmas conference. The reporter wisely said nothing, letting the visuals say it all.

Jennie confided she wanted a proper dollhouse for her favorite dolly, which she proudly displayed for Santa's inspection, to make sure he got the right size, and a new coffeemaker for her mother. Ben nodded and signed that he would do his very best to get her what she wanted because she'd been a very good girl.

Jennie's mother knew sign, and once Ben had finished with the girl the mom gave him a hard look. "Why would you promise her all them things? I don't have that kind of money, not for the dollhouse she wants! Isn't it enough she gets made fun of by the other children without you making her promises I can't keep?"

"Please, ma'am," Ben said. "I work at Hurley's. Go there tomorrow and ask for Moira in Housewares, and she'll get you a coffeemaker. And there'll be a dollhouse too—if not, a gift certificate. On me." He winked. "Just tell Moira ... well tell her that Santa sent you." He smiled down at Jennie. "She reminds me of my sister. I haven't seen in too long. I think she just helped me decide what I'm giving myself for Christmas this year." He winked at the little girl. *"See you soon,"* he signed. *"Christmas!"*

The next day, Ben went to the toy department and picked out a dollhouse just the right size for a very special dolly of a very special little girl. He noted the price, then tracked down Moira and gave her a blank, signed check.

"What's this, then?" Moira asked. "You won the Lotto, have you?"

"Better than that, though I can't explain it now. A woman is going to ask for you today and say that Santa sent her. I want you to give her whatever coffeemaker she picks out and add that amount to the price for this model dollhouse." He showed her the name and price. "Then wish her a Merry Christmas from me."

Moira looked at him, smiled, then to his surprise she kissed him on the cheek. "I think you're starting to believe, Santa." She took the check, but before she turned to go, added, "And I am, too. Care to join me for lunch tomorrow? I know where we can find some good meatloaf."

"It's a date, meatloaf or not."

Jennie's mom came in shortly after opening and came by Santa Land on her way out, hefting a bag in each hand. She didn't join the line but waved and mouthed a "thank-you," before making her way out of the store.

The rest of the evening was a blur. When the last child had been seen and the doors were locked, Ben rose slowly from the throne, wished his faithful elves a good night, and limped to the locker room. There, taped to his locker, was a note from Mike: "See me before you go home."

Ben changed out of his costume, and as he rode the elevator to the top floor, he reviewed everything he'd done for the past three days to try to figure out what he'd done now. Whatever it was, it didn't involve drinking on the job. He'd even avoided using mouthwash for fear someone would mistake the odor for booze. The bell chimed, the door opened, and he squared his shoulders. Best get this over with.

He knocked, and Mike called him in. Ben found the store manager sitting at his desk smiling. Ben relaxed a hair.

"I hear you've been moonlighting, Ben. Why didn't you tell me?"

"I'm sorry, Mike. If you're talking about the food bank, it was a charity event. I wasn't paid anything, and I reported to work on time. And the costume I used belongs to the car dealership I work for. I hope that's not a problem, I ... How'd you hear about it, anyway?"

Mike's smile widened another notch. "I meant, why didn't you tell me you can sign? As for how did I find out? Ben, it's all over the local news! And my sister in New Jersey said it's even gone nationwide! The film of you and that little girl has made you both rock stars. What did she ask for, by the way?"

"A coffeemaker for her mom and a dollhouse. I paid for them, and the mom picked them up at the store this afternoon."

Mike stood and walked around his desk before offering his hand. As the two of them shook, Mike said, "Ben, you've got this job every season as long as you want it."

"Well ... yeah, I like it here. Maybe I'll take you up on that."

Danny was watching TV as Emily made supper when the segment about the food drive came on. He stared for a minute, then ... "Mom! Come quick! Is that?"

Emily walked in, wiping her hands, and froze as the reporter's voice continued, "A very special little girl got a special visit today from the man in red." The video played on of Jennie's face becoming more animated as she and Ben signed back and forth, then the mother and him, then the mother's hug and Jennie kissing Ben on the cheek before the camera cut back to the reporter interviewing the mother after.

"Hello, ma'am, do you have just a minute?"

"Yes, yes, of course," the woman answered as she brushed away her tears.

"Can we ask Jennie what she and Santa talked about?"

Jennie and her mom went back and forth for a minute. "She said that it's between her and Santa, but she said it was good. Really good."

The camera cut back to the reporter. "And there you have it, just another Christmas miracle here in San Antonio, where it appears Christmas wishes still come true."

Danny's mouth had slowly opened wider and wider as the segment played on. When it was over, he looked up. "Mom, was that ...?"

Emily found another use for her kitchen towel before answering. "Yes, Danny. That was your dad."

Eleven

When he got home, Ben found a text on his phone from Susan.

Good job, Santa. I hope you remember us little people now that you're famous. Don't forget it's all because you had me as a sister to train you right!

Ben smiled and carefully tapped out his response: *How about I come visit after Christmas, and you can remind me in person? It's been too long.*

It had been too long. Jennie had reminded him of that.

The next day, Ben found a smiling Moira waiting for him in the break room.

"Good day, Santa," she said. "I hope you're not too famous to have some humble meatloaf with the likes of me."

"Well, you have been a good girl, so sure, why not? On me!"

She laughed. "Oh, a big spender, are you? I could get used to that!"

"I'm sorry if I was a little insensitive last time. I—"

"Oh, get aways. No, I'm sorry. I do actually have a cat—I'd forgotten to feed her! That's why I had to get off so quick."

Ben chuckled. "Ah. I thought …"

"And then it was all crazy-busy days, wasn't it." She smiled. "Crazy days for crazy ladies, eh?"

Moira noticed Ben wasn't wearing his wedding ring anymore. She didn't say anything, but her smile got a wee bit wider.

Christmas Day had come at last! Ben drove over to the house, still a little nervous as to what reaction he would get. But he was welcomed inside, gifts were exchanged, and a date to see the spy movie with Danny and Steve was made for the next day.

"You've changed," Emily said to him in the kitchen, the boys nosily playing a video game on the TV on the lounge.

"Have I?

"You're looking outward again. Looking out for others. Much more the man I married."

Ben nodded and found himself smiling.

He drove home, lighter than he'd felt for a year. Maybe more. *Maybe Christmas gifts come in threes*, he mused. A day out with Danny, a trip to see Susan, and a date with Moira in the New Year.

He pulled into his trailer park and eased the car to a stop. He grabbed the bag of little gifts he'd gotten and put his key in the lock of his doublewide. Pulling himself in, he placed the bag on the floor and went to the fridge for a soda. That was when he noticed a small box on his counter with a Christmas card attached. He looked around: everything seemed in order. Then he caught it—the faint whiff of cookies.

He opened the card, which read:

Mrs. Claus told me of your good work, Ben. Thank you! Nowadays we need all the help we can get. I think the suit fits you very well, and I hope you are one of us for many Christmases to come (ho, ho, ho!).

S. Claus

Inside the box were three candles, labeled "Danny," "Susan," and "Moira." He gently lifted them out. Another candle was nestled underneath. Its label read "Ben."

Twelve

Someplace very far north, the wind blew as fresh snow fell on the ice. Deep below the prying eyes of satellites, elves smiled as candles from people who'd seen a Christmas miracle on the news flickered back to life.

"You did well with Ben, my dear."

Mrs. Claus looked up and smiled at her husband. "All those games Ben watched his son. Danny didn't even know his dad was there, but still Ben came. Patience, endurance, willingness ... Ben's spark never truly went out. He just let 'life' smother it. But it was always there. And Moira spotted it too ... I have a feeling about those two."

"Hm. Perhaps next year, I'll be dropping in on them in Ireland."

Mrs. Claus patted her husband on the chest. "You look beat, dear. Fancy some cocoa before you turn in?"

Santa smiled. "It's what makes it all worthwhile."

"The sparks that light the candles? Or the cocoa?"

"Oh, both." Santa stretched and yawned, taking the mug Mrs. C offered. "Mmm, definitely both," he said, sipping a well-earned reward.

WHAT SANTA HAS TAUGHT ME

BRADLEY HARPER

After I retired from the Army (37 years, 4 months, and 9 days—and yes, someone WAS counting!), I grew a beard because, hey, I could! It came out white, which at my age was no surprise. But then my wife began hinting that I should get a job as Santa. I was surprised at her suggestion but recalled that, when she was eight, she decided she wanted to marry Santa Claus. Now, if she was to become Mrs. Claus ... You get the idea.

So, I auditioned for a local park, and to my surprise, and more than a small amount of panic, I got one of the slots. *Now I was in for it ...*

I began walking through the toy section of stores. I memorized "The Night Before Christmas." And, as I speak various languages (to differing degrees of proficiency), I memorized how to say "What would you like for Christmas?" in Spanish, French, Italian, and German (the park gets a fair number of international visitors). I didn't have to understand the reply: a smile and a knowing wink are universal.

Day three on the throne ... I got this! And it's kinda fun. As long as I don't promise more than "I'll look into it," I'm golden.

Then life, as it is known to do, threw Santa-me a curveball. One of the young ladies serving as an elf comes up to me and says, "Santa, you're about to see three kids. They've been orphans for the past year. The foster parents keeping them have just been approved to adopt them, and um ... well, they want YOU to tell them!"

I took a deep breath, and there they were. No pressure, right? The girl was the oldest. Around twelve, she was obviously a non-believer by now, but playing along for her younger brothers. The ten-year-old was unsure. That phase where they don't really think you're real but don't want to blow their chances ... just in case. The eight-year-old still had faith. His eyes large, brown, and round.

Unsure what to say at that moment, I fell back on the old stand-by, "What would you like for Christmas?" They said something, but honestly, I didn't hear a word, thinking to myself, *What can I say? What CAN I say?*

Then it came to me. I took another deep breath and said, "Those are great ideas. I'll look into it, but I have something for you today."

"What's that, Santa?" the oldest asked, obviously the spokesman for the group.

"A family," I said.

They looked puzzled, but when I explained they would not have to leave the foster family, that they would all grow up together, well, there wasn't a dry eye in the house. (Yeah, I teared up just now, again.)

So what did I learn? In the Hero's Journey, the Hero comes back changed by their Quest. Though I didn't leave my throne, I had just been on quite a ride.

I learned that I wanted to be Santa Claus more than anything else in the world. I fully embraced the role after that. Santa has made me a kinder, more patient man. With my beard, I stand out anywhere I go. Which means, I have to be careful about what I say and how I act as I never know where or when a child might see me. I have to be in tune with "the better angels of my nature," whenever I'm in public. (OK, I can't eat ribs in public anymore. But it's worth it!)

So Santa has made me a better person. When I put on my superhero costume and go forth to fight for happiness, I never promise a toy, but I always offer a hug.

I have a photo of my backside as I'm hugging an elderly gentleman. His name was Walter, and I met him at a gift exchange at an Alzheimer's daycare center. Every patient got a gift bag selected for them by the staff, and I handed them out and hugged each resident. Walter's face is beaming in the picture, and a trick of the lighting perhaps ... *perhaps*, but there is a small halo around his head.

I got the photo from his daughter, who tracked me down. She said her dad was abandoned by his family as a small child and never had a visit from Santa his entire life.

The next year, I was told that Walter had passed. His daughter told the director of the daycare center that the photo of me hugging him had become his favorite, and at his funeral, she had that picture blown up and placed on an easel beside his open coffin.

That taught me how powerful even one moment can be in another person's life. Don't hold back ... *this* moment may never come again.

The Greek philosopher Heraclitus once said that a man can never cross a river twice, for each time both he and the river will have changed. Every time I assume the role, it may be the first time for whoever I come into contact with. I may define Santa for the rest of their life.

No pressure, right? But here's the thing. Just like Dumbo and his magic feather, the magic is not in the robe; it was inside me all the time. I just needed the license that the costume gave me to tap into it.

You may not wear a red suit, but I hereby deputize you to share love and joy, wherever you go. You can do it. Find that better angel that has been inside you all along, and let them breathe.

You, and all those around you, will be the better for it.

Happy holidays and Merry Christmas to one and all,

Brad

Bradley Harper
Bio

"When an Army Pathologist retires, naturally he goes back to school to get a degree in writing ..."

Bradley Harper is a retired US Army Colonel and pathologist with extensive experience in autopsies and forensic investigation. Along with clinical experience, he had four commands, and is the only non-Italian to ever receive the Knights of Malta award for his support of the Italian Army. A lifelong fan of Sherlock Holmes, upon retirement he received his *Associates in Creative Writing* from Full Sail University, to help him write the book *A Knife in the Fog* that he'd always wanted to read. Harper did intensive research for his debut novel, which involved a young Doctor Conan Doyle in the hunt for Jack the Ripper, including a trip to London's East End with noted Jack the Ripper historian Richard Jones.

A Knife in the Fog was published in October 2018 and was a finalist for a 2019 Edgar Award by the Mystery Writers of America for Best First Novel by an American Author and is a Recommended Read by the Arthur Conan Doyle Estate.

Knife went on to win Killer Nashville's 2019 Silver Falchion as Best Mystery. The audio book, narrated by former Royal Shakespearean actor Matthew Lloyd Davies, won Audiofile Magazine's 2019 Earphone award for Best Mystery and Suspense. The book is also available in Japan via Hayakawa Publishing.

His second novel, *Queen's Gambit*, involving a fictional assassination attempt on Queen Victoria, won Killer Nashville's 2020 Silver Falchion Award twice, once for Best Suspense, and again as Book of the Year.

BIBLIOGRAPHY:
- *A Knife in the Fog*, Seventh Street Books, 2018
- *Queen's Gambit*, Seventh Street Books, 2019

Each Christmas, Dr. Harper takes a break from the authorial life, when he and his wife—to whom he has been married for 45 years—portray a happily married couple from the North Pole.

Find Brad's books on

Amazon

Visit Brad's website for news about his activities

www.bharperauthor.com

Follow Brad on social media

**Twitter, Instagram, Goodreads, and Facebook:
@bharperauthor**

The Bells of Christmas II

CALLING US HOME:
AN IRISH CHRISTMAS

MARIA O'ROURKE

C hristmas in Ireland is the highlight of the year.
We love to gather, and as an island country on the edge of Europe, Christmas is the giant magnet that draws Irish people home from around the world. For two weeks prior to the big day, Dublin airport is a riot of activity with children running to greet relatives with banners, hugs, and tears. There are fairy lights and music, carol singers, Santas, cribs.

Christmas gives us the perfect excuse to forget everything bad in the world and just be children again.

I've always loved Christmas. It's something visceral, as if all the happy childhood memories are captured in the smell of whiskey-laden pudding and pine needles. My mother made Christmas pudding in a big, brown ceramic mixing bowl with a white interior. When the mixture was ready, she'd invite us all to stir it with a wooden spoon while making a wish. Mine was usually about the gifts I hoped to get on Christmas morning, and the aroma of the pudding boiling heightened those fantasies all the more. Nutmeg and cinnamon, candied peel, suet, whiskey, and stout. The recipe itself was pure poetry, and the art of tying the top with greaseproof paper and twine in an intricate loop felt like putting the finishing touches to the Mona Lisa.

Like all Irish families, we had Christmas rituals, and one of the most important in our house was the visit of my grandmother on the Sunday before Christmas. "Granny O" was my father's mother—the "O" was to distinguish her from the other granny who lived with us. Granny O's visit was heralded for weeks, and the excitement surrounding it was breathtaking.

In preparation for her arrival, the Christmas tree had to be decorated, holly sprigs placed behind all the pictures, cards arranged on strings around the walls, and the crib set up on the hall table with a tea-light candle in front of it. There were no half-measures when it came to Christmas with Granny O. Her own house was a veritable Santa's grotto, and we had to compete! Straight after lunch, Dad would drive over to collect her, and we could hardly breathe with excitement until we saw the sweep of his car pulling into the drive again.

With our faces pressed to the window, our hearts sank every time the wrong car passed, and then finally ... *finally!* we'd race to the door, sizing up the shapes of parcels and boxes, wondering what they could possibly hold. Large, neat presents, oddly shaped packages, and black sacks tied with colored streamers. I could hardly bear the suspense when she'd stop to admire the crib in the hall. We squealed and pulled at her with tiny hands until she finally took up her position in the armchair by the fire in the sitting room.

And then the unwrapping would begin. I remember crying dolls, ironing boards, tea sets, Lego, and board games. Each year brought its own treasures. Neatly written gift-tags were read out to shouts of delight and paper ripping. By the time all the presents were open, the floor was littered with torn paper, bags, and ribbons. In my memory it was every bit as good as Christmas morning, which was exactly what Granny O wanted.

When all the excitement was over, it was time to give Granny O her gift. It was usually a cardigan or slippers, although one year I remember we gave her a "Super Ser" gas heater. It was huge and it took a whole roll of wrapping paper to cover it. Granny O's reaction was always the same. She would go completely quiet. Her thin, age-mottled hands took an age to rip off the Sellotape while we studied her face for the flicker of a reaction.

Then the tears would come. "If only I had *him*," she would say—he being my grandfather, who had died suddenly the year I was born. She never got a present without wishing he was there to share it. Embarrassed by the emotion, we'd drift off to play with this year's gifts, anticipating our friends' jealous faces when they'd call round to play that evening, and my mother would rush to get her a cup of tea.

As we got older, Granny O brought cassettes, records, and perfume, but whatever the gift was, it had to be exactly the one you wanted. I gradually understood that secret conversations must have taken place in the preceding weeks to ensure that our reactions were nothing short of pure joy. This routine was repeated in our cousins' houses too, and Granny O, who was one of fifteen children herself and never saw such opulence in childhood, reveled in the joy of giving.

Once Granny O's visit had passed, it was time to look forward to Santa Claus. In the week leading up to Christmas, we were brought to visit Santa in a local department store. We knew he wasn't the *real deal* and that he was just a *helper* Santa, but we trusted him to pass on our secret desires for what we wanted under the tree on Christmas morning. Sitting on his knee for a few moments was a necessary ordeal so you could whisper the request into his ear. He was hot and sweaty and it was good to get out of there, but there was a sense that the wheels had been set in motion and we had reason to hope.

On Christmas morning, as soon as one of us children woke up, we'd run into my parents' room and Dad would go downstairs first to check if Santa had arrived. By the time he called us to come down, he had the fire lit and the Christmas tree lights on.

Racing down in our nightclothes, we pushed each other through the sitting-room door where piles of presents surrounded the tree. Conveniently, Santa always wrote "R" on the bundle for Ruth, "M" on my bundle, and "J" on Jane's. He knew how to prevent a row! I remember the mixture of delight and relief because, although we never actually met a child who got a bag of coal, we were reliably told that was what a bold child would get. And you just never knew!

One of my best Santa presents ever was a typewriter. It was blue and white and had a real ink-ribbon in it. He forgot to give me any paper, so I had to root around the house and write on the back of letters and flyers. But I could pretend to be a secretary or a writer or an official in the government. I typed urgent letters to my parents and a set of rules for my bedroom. Then I started to write my own adventure series. I say "series" ... I didn't get past the first chapter. It took ages, with two fingers and paper that kept getting stuck, but it was magical.

One year, my sister and I got red mini-projectors. There was a small wheel with slides of "The Aristocats" and "Tom and Jerry." When you turned on the bulb and inserted the wheel, you could see the slide on the wall and click it forward to the next slide. We were enthralled! It was like the cinema! And when we finally got tired of the slides, we used them as the footlights for one of our "shows," where we charged our parents to come and listen to us sing, dance, and tell silly jokes, stepping out dramatically from the spotlight on the sitting-room curtains.

I'll never forget the Christmas Eve my sister got three teeth taken out under gas. They were only baby teeth and I really resented all the attention she was getting. But it was nothing to the rage I felt on Christmas morning, when there was an extra present under the tree for her from Santa! Who knew Santa could be so unfair! I mean, my teeth were fine, but I would have had them taken out if I'd known that there was a giant art set going!

Generally, though, I had a good relationship with Santa. We were always told that he could see if you were being good or bad, and that was a bit worrying. What with the threat of coal always in the back of our minds. But he mustn't have been looking when I "accidentally" hit my sister with a hatchet. There was only a tiny mark on her head afterwards, but she made *such* a fuss about it. She insisted on wearing a giant plaster for a whole week. But Santa must have been busy that week, because I still got a toy guitar for Christmas and that was exactly what I wanted.

After all the present-opening, there was only time for a hurried breakfast before we bundled into the car for Christmas Morning Mass in our local church. Wearing our best Christmas outfits, we trooped into the pews, sometimes sneaking a small toy in with us for entertainment. There were babies in arms, coats with fur trimming, Christmas jumpers and dresses. It was as if the excitement from all the houses in the town had been bottled and brought to this special place to celebrate the birth of the baby in the crib. The choir sang "Away in a Manger" and "Once in Royal David's City," and we all joined in.

Christmas dinner was always turkey and ham in our house. We bought them oven-ready from the butcher's. Not so my friend next door: Jenny Murphy and her family had a turkey hanging upside down under the stairs for a week before Christmas—with the head *still on*! It was disgusting! Although we couldn't stop looking at his scrawny neck and blood-shot eyes and poking his pimpled skin. Where food came from was pretty much a mystery to me, and that's the way I wanted it to stay, having seen the Murphys' turkey.

Every Christmas, we ate in the "dining room." Although that was what we called it, this was the only day we ate there in the entire year! The table was extended to its full size by means of a lever underneath the middle panel and pulled to the center of the floor. I can still see it now, with candles and Christmas crackers merrily decorating a starched white cloth. My mother always set it the night before, and, as children, we would repeatedly go in to check if there was anything else we could add to make it even more perfect. Rare treats in our house (reserved for *special* occasions), red lemonade and Coca-Cola bottles graced the center. Tall glasses for the children and sparkly wine goblets for the adults, tablemats, silver cutlery, cranberry sauce, and mustard. With serviettes flamboyantly arranged at each place, the stage was set and ready for the annual drama to unfold.

Unlike other women at the time, my mother wasn't overly fond of cooking. She didn't bake bread, for example; nor did she sew, as my friends' mothers did. We didn't come home from school to hearty stews and apple pies. In fact, mostly I was reared on ready-tocook pancakes, tins of mashed potato, and Spam. Yet, I didn't feel in the least disadvantaged. In fact, I felt a bit sorry for my friends, who had to eat … *vegetables*. I even tried to avoid eating meals in their houses in case they'd expect me to eat greens too. I almost threw up once when a neighbor insisted I try Brussels sprouts, and when I first saw something strange known as "spaghetti," I went home and told my mother the neighbors were eating worms. My friends raved about chicken casseroles and bacon with cabbage, but I was more familiar with a tinned steak-and-kidney pie than a Sunday roast.

But Christmas dinner … That was different, though. And probably all the more special for the fact that home-cooked family meals *chez nous* were rare. I was the middle child of three girls, with one sister close in age and the other nine years younger. So, along with my parents, and the grandmother who lived with us, we were six in all. Finally, the time would come for us to sit around the table, with Granny at one end, Dad at the other. My mother would be the last to sit down (there was always something just about to burn on the cooker). Then Dad would say grace, which was quite a performance and tended to go on longer than any of we children could tolerate. Finally, I'd be picking up my cutlery and giving him an exasperated look, only to get a withering stare from my mother. If Dad's grace had gone on for an hour, my mother would have looked interested! When, *finally*, we were free to sample the turkey, ham, and roast potatoes, they were all the more welcome.

I've never understood why people like Christmas pudding. In fact, none of the traditional Christmas desserts are to my taste. A traditional Irish pudding is dark brown in color, laden with dried fruit and moistened with Guinness. It's best served warm with brandy poured on the top and set alight, the blue flame adding a touch of excitement before it's doused in brandy custard. Actually, alcohol was always a chief ingredient in our Christmas desserts! Pudding and the other traditional dessert, trifle, which has the sponge soaked in sherry. And finally, Christmas cake seasoned with whiskey. Or brandy. Or rum. Or port. Or all four! While my family was gorging on these rich Christmas treats, I would enjoy a bowl of ice cream, with me by then itching to get away from the table to watch "Billy Smart's Family Circus" on TV.

As my sister and I became teenagers, Christmas changed, although having a sister so much younger than us meant we kept the magic alive for her. By then my grandmother's mind was getting confused and she constantly spoke about people who were long dead and wanted to go "home." Home to a house that no longer existed. We jollied her along with Christmas music and stories, and she still enjoyed the predictability of the customs she had known since childhood.

Gradually the gifts under the tree changed from colorful toys to musical instruments and perfume, records, and clothes. We made lists rather than writing to Santa, agonizing over them for weeks But still there was always something we hadn't asked for, a surprise that would draw forth a "wow!" or a "no way!" Although we had to remember not to say "Thanks, Mam and Dad," in front of my younger sister. We were as excited as she was to see her new bike or ball or scooter, her enthusiasm electrifying the room.

When I was thirteen, I got a tape-recorder, and I thought I was the luckiest girl in the world. I think I gasped when I saw the shiny image on its box. It was a deliciously crisp chrome and a deep, beautiful black with a retractable handle. When you pressed the eject button the little door opened really slowly. *And* there was a built-in microphone. That Christmas, my older sister and I stayed up to listen to the "Top 100" on Radio Luxembourg. As soon as a song we liked was announced, we pressed "play" and "record" together—in perfect sync—and stayed perfectly quiet until it was over. It was such a thrill to be able to capture our favorite music and play it back whenever we wanted. It was like capturing the wind. We used to put a sign on the door that read "Recording in Progress: DO NOT ENTER!" and screeched at anyone who did.

While the excitement of Christmas Eve was never quite as intense as when we were children, new traditions emerged that were like rites of passage to the grown-up world. It was around this time that we were introduced to Midnight Mass. Now old enough to stay awake late, my mother brought my older sister and me out into the hushed Christmas Eve air to make our way to the church, while Dad stayed at home with my sleeping younger sister and Granny. People were walking from all directions, calling out "Happy Christmas!" to each other, even if it was a half-hour premature. Inside the church, the crib was set up with an empty manger, ready for the baby Jesus to be born, and the choir sang "O Come All Ye Faithful" as the priest proceeded up the aisle, holding the infant aloft. The stained glass looked so different with no light coming through from outside.

We felt like we were part of the Christmas story.

These days, the gifts under the tree for my own children seem much more sophisticated. iPhones and PlayStations, AirPods and drones. And yet, the Christmas spirit is the same. It has been a joy to pass on the Christmas traditions, and now, many years later, I find myself doing exactly the same thing my parents did, and their parents before them. On December 25, we will eat turkey and ham and gather around the tree.

Just as we always did.

We'll go to Midnight Mass and put a candle in the window as a symbol of welcome.

Just as we did years before.

The years come, and they go. Children grow up, and life sometimes gets out of hand.

But there always was, there still is—and there *always will be*—Christmas to call us home. Christmas to steady the ship and remind us of what we hold dear.

Maria O'Rourke
Bio

After a career in teaching spanning thirty years, Maria O'Rourke is now a full-time writer, having completed a Masters in Creative Writing at the University of Limerick in Ireland. She draws on her own challenges in personal, work, and family life to bring out what is universal in each individual experience. Writing both prose and poetry, her favorite genre is creative non-fiction. She has recently been awarded the Wild Atlantic Writing Award for this genre as well as being shortlisted for the Anthology Short Fiction Competition, The Farnham Flash Fiction Competition, and the Liberties Press Humorous Short Story Competition. She has been published by *The Blue Nib* and *The Ogham Stone*. Mother to three grown-up children, she lives in Carlow, Ireland, with her husband, David.

You can read about Maria and see some of her work on her website mariaorourke.com.

THE BEAR'S
LAST WORD ON THE MATTER

WILL KNIGHT

"Would you like an adventure now," he said casually ...
"or would you like to have your tea first?"

– J.M. Barrie, *Peter Pan*

Now
James

A dvancing years beset each and everyone eventually, James knew, though he preferred to view the passage of time as experiences on his journey. Only, it wasn't his journey that was soon to reach its final destination. It was his friend's.

So perhaps now it was time to tell his story.

Flurries of snow flickered in the wind outside as he removed and dusted off his beanie, attending to it as one might a top hat at the ball. It was a gift last Christmas from his sister, Hayley. A pity she couldn't come today. His friend loved being doted on by her.

The building he'd entered was quite modern really; and quite warm—cozy even, he decided as he unbuttoned his winter wax jacket.

James sighed at what lay before him. One of his last visits to his childhood friend, no longer in rude health. Well, who likely is when they live in a care home? Yes, advancing years beset each and everyone. Not even his extraordinary childhood friend could overcome that.

Placing his beanie in his lower-left pocket, James blew into his hands, to warm them or to perhaps set himself for the task at hand. It would be bittersweet, but it might be fun, too, to remember the old days. Those days when he and his best buddy had lived all those adventures. Had *done* stuff. Stuff that didn't involve sitting at a computer, designing ... whatever he was asked in the brief.

Banks ... not exactly the most exciting clients. Which didn't exactly lend itself to being the most exciting life these days.

James looked up from wiping his feet on the mat. There she was, signaling him.

Now

Jess

She'd actually been the one to take the call in the office of the local newspaper. Well, it was her job, alongside being head reporter. And photocopier and coffeemaker. He had a story, maybe, he'd said. Might be good at Christmastime, he'd said. Be nice for kids to read about the main man.

"Main man?" she'd asked.

"Yeah, you know. Captain Christmas."

"Captain Christmas. As in ... some new Marvel movie?"

The man chuckled. "Sorry, no. I mean the jolly fat guy that brings all the presents and things."

"Ah, Santa Claus."

"Yeah. Santa Claus."

Jess reached for her coffee cup, knocked it, and spilled its long-since-cold contents onto some papers. Oh well, nothing for it. She swept the liquid off with the arm of her sweater. Her *ridiculous* sweater. Who in their right mind would wear a sweater with such a crazy jolly fat guy in red on it? Reporters desperate for Holiday-season stories, that's who.

"Funny how folks always assume Santa is jolly at this time of year. I would have thought he'd be pretty stressed out every December," Jess said, wiping the excess liquid off her arm, the phone cricked into her neck.

"Well, he can be a bit," the man said. "But mostly he's pretty cool. And jolly."

"I see. And you'd know this how ...?"

"I met him."

And now she sat in the waiting room of this care home, waiting for a surely ridiculous story. Her attention was caught by the movement of someone entering the building. That might be him. The young man who claimed to have lived fantastic adventures with a ... with a, well, a companion that defied belief.

Jess noted the man's reluctance to enter. She lifted a still damp arm and waved at him. She noticed a big smile spread across his face. A face that was round and appealing. Eyes that crinkled into the smile. And hair that refused to obey as he attempted to pat it down after removing his cap.

"Alright?" he said as he approached, his arm outstretched. "James Chapman."

"Jessica Walter. Pleased to meet you, Mr. Chapman."

"James, please. I don't want to get confused with my dad, Joseph."

His easy smile was warming. "Jess. Not to be confused with my mother, Mary, I hope."

James nodded.

"So ... look, I hope you don't mind ... I mean, I came mainly because the day was quiet. Not much going on right now. People are mainly interested in shopping and partying. No one actually does anything much else that's worth reporting on."

"That's fine. I wasn't going to call in. But if I don't do it now, then ... well, this is probably my last chance to. And it's cool if you don't believe my story. I'm not really doing it for you or anyone else. It's for my friend."

"Your ... *friend*."

"Yeah. Come on, I'll introduce you."

Now

James

james knocked gently on the door and opened it a crack. He peered in. The bed was empty, made neatly. Not by his friend, he doubted. No one changed from being so messy to being neat and tidy. At least, he hoped not.

He stuck his head inside the crack. And there he was on the sofa by the window, which resembled something of a wide cinema screen showing a nature documentary from Patagonia in winter. The snow danced behind his friend, who slowly and stiffly sat up and smiled.

Damn, he looks ... old. Even more so than when he'd visited last week.

"James!"

"Alright?"

Now

Jess

🔔 🔔 🔔

Jess followed James into the room.

What the ...?!

There he was, this special childhood friend. Just as James had claimed. Sitting on the sofa at the end of the smallish room was ... was a bear.

Unbelievably an actual *bear*. A little one. Maybe three feet tall? Round head, shaggy fur, gray as an old man's beard.

"Wh-what is this?" she stumbled out.

"My friend," James said. "Like I told you."

"But ... But h-he's a—"

"Bear, okay if we come in and chat?"

"Of course it is!"

Jess watched the bear take off a pair of half-lensed reading glasses and set his book aside. James moved easily inside and went to hug his friend, who struggled down—with a soft groan, she heard—from his sofa perch to stand on two ... paws ... to embrace his friend.

"What are you reading, mate?" James asked the little bear.

"Arabian Knights."

"Ah ... like the time we ..."

"Mm."

Jess watched them a moment before James turned around to her and said, "Come on in, Jess. Bear doesn't bite. Much."

Jess swallowed and let out the breath she'd been holding.

"Oi!" The bear playfully swiped at James's arm before struggling back onto the sofa, accepting a helping hand to do so. "I've never bitten anyone in my life! Only Penguins."

"Y-you eat penguins?!"

James laughed. "Only the chocolate ones. As many as he can get his hands on."

The bear smiled. "You didn't happen to ...?"

"Got some cake, yes."

"I want! Mmm ..."

Jess brushed a lock of auburn hair from her eye. "I-I ... Is this ... Are you ..."

"Real?" the bear finished.

"Well, um, yes."

The little bear lifted an arm and smelled his fur. "I stink, therefore I am."

Despite herself, Jess smiled at the bear's smile, writ large across his round head. Honestly, looking at him more closely now, if she had to describe the creature—and she would have to, of course—she'd say he looked like one of those bears off greetings cards.

The bear eagerly took one of the individual cakes James offered. He unwrapped it like a past master and broke a piece off. "Cake, Jess?"

"No, no, thank you. I don't usually accept treats from, um, bears. At least, not on a first meeting."

"Ah, I'm sure," the bear said, nodding. "Well, more for me! So, take your coat off. You can hang it over ... um ... gosh, where's that coat hook gone?"

"It's right over there, Bear," James said. "Here, Jess, let me hang that for you." James shed his own coat in an easy fluid motion and hung both on the hook in the opposite corner.

"Come sit beside me," the bear said. "Or ... opposite if you prefer?"

"Um ... yes, maybe over here is better."

"Ah, yes, of course. Put the kettle on, James? Fancy a cuppa, Jess?"

"You drink tea?"

"It's been known."

"Been known!" James snickered. "He used to insist on tea at teatime, on the dot, every day! Got to have your afternoon cuppa, eh, Bear!"

"The Turks call it *Keyif zahmanah*. It sort of comes to mean 'your time for you—something nice to enjoy.' I don't speak Turkish or anything. Not the modern version, anyway. More the old Ottoman ... from when we were there."

Jess shot him a glance.

Now

James

James stirred the pot of tea again and then poured it into three waiting mugs. "I see they've given you the Rudolph ones again this year, mate."

"Heat-change ones, James," Bear said. "Kind of cool. Or hot, I think I mean. Anyway ... Oh, thank you," he said, taking the mug James offered. "You didn't bring any cake or anything, did you?"

James watched as Bear took the mug gently but firmly, noting how much attention Bear now had to give to the task. "There's some right there, I see."

"Oh! Yummy."

Jess flipped open a notebook. And tapped a pen on the blank page. "I'm not sure where to start ... Maybe I could ask you where you came from ... Mr. Bear?"

"Just Bear. Don't want to be confused with my father." He winked.

James smiled and sipped his brew.

"An unusual name," Jess said.

Bear nodded and sipped his tea. "Blame him," he said, inclining his head to James.

"I, erm, lacked imagination in those days," James replied.

"Where did you come from, Bear?" Jess asked, her pen poised above the snow-white paper for the exposé.

"I dunno where I came from all those years ago. I just woke up one day. In James's bedroom."

James watched Jess scribble down a note. She looked up at him.

"Oh, sorry. Don't ask me. I was pretty young then. I just thought he was a cool Christmas present."

"Turns out this bear was for life, not just for Christmas, eh," Jess said.

James looked away. Not for life, no. He covered his reaction by sipping his tea.

"So ... I can't believe I'm going to ask this as a serious question, but given what—sorry, *who* is before me, I will. Tell me, did you really meet Santa Claus? *The* Santa Claus?"

"Oh, yes! Of course. Twice, actually!" Bear said, his pride evident.

And why not? How many could say they had met Santa Claus?

"And what were the circumstances in which you both met him?"

"Ah," said Bear. "The first time—now *that's* a story, eh, James?"

James smiled widely. "It is."

"You should have listened to me! I told you we'd find trouble!"

"You were right, I admit it." They gently clinked mugs together.

"So ..." prompted Jess.

"So?" asked Bear.

"So tell me the story. I'd love to hear it."

"A story? You want a story, do you? James, let's tell her one of the Christmas adventures we had, shall we? We met Santa Claus, Jezz." Bear put his paw to the side of his nose. "Hush, hush. Don't tell anyone. Except for your readers, of course."

Jess looked at James, and he immediately got her unasked question. He nodded slightly, looked away. Bear was increasingly having problems holding onto the immediate present.

"We saved Christmas, Jess," Bear proclaimed. He broke off a piece of cake and put it nonchalantly into his mouth. Pleasure spread across his face.

James's heart winced. Just enjoy the time here and now, he told himself.

"That's quite an achievement, Bear," Jess said. "I'd love to hear more."

"We might need two pots for this," Bear said and sipped his tea. He looked at Jess and said, "Pen ready?"

"It is."

"Well, here goes. 'The elves were dead, to begin with ...'"

"Come again...?"

"Bear! Stop stealing from Dickens," James said, chuckling.

"You read Dickens?" Jess asked, incredulous.

"Um, yes?"

"Muppet Christmas Carol," James said.

"Ah, of course."

"Best ever Christmas movie!" Bear proclaimed. "But not quite as good as actually saving Christmas ..."

Then

Bear

It was Christmas Eve morning, the last morning before Christmas, and James, Hayley, and I were thinking of all the presents we'd be getting tomorrow. We all reckoned we'd been a good boy, girl, and bear this year. Okay, James was kind of hoping that incident with the dustbin wasn't important. And the carpet stuffed inside it wasn't that magic, not really. Besides, that was way back in the summer anyway, so it didn't count.

"I wish it could be Christmas Day every day ..." I didn't realize I was singing it until I noticed James and Hayley had covered their ears. "Was I—"

"Out of tune again?" James said. "Only a lot."

"Oh, sorry." I looked over at the large Christmas tree by the window. Its beautiful lights gently flashed and sparkled in rhythm to the soft Christmas music they were playing. And underneath, spread neatly around, sat a huge pile of beautifully wrapped presents. Tempting tags announced their names. Big ones, little ones in red wrapping, green wrapping ... well, you get the point. The presents looked *really* inviting. But they were for tomorrow, Christmas Day. Which was simply still *ages* away.

Then I noticed James was gazing at one of the silver baubles on the tree. I jumped down off the sofa and went up to it, James following, and looked at the bauble. Was that some kind of face forming within it?

It blinked.

"Hello ... hello?" the little face said, trying to see out properly. "Can yous all sees me?"

"Er ... yes ..." James replied.

"Well, that be right good."

"*Grinley?*" I asked.

"Ha-ha, I be right glad that yous are rememberin' me! Hello!"

"Grinley! How did you get inside the little bauble?" James asked.

"Oh, I don't be insides of 'ere really. Santa's asked mees to contact yous. Wees be needin' your 'elp!"

"Why, what's wrong?" I asked.

"There be no times for explainin' now. Santa'll tell yous everythin' when yous gets 'ere." Grinley's face began to fade.

"Wait! Tell us what?" James asked.

"Wees gotta saves Christmas. There be no times to lose!"

Now

James

"Who's Grinley?" Jess asked us.

"The head elf, of course!" Bear replied, his memory of years back still pin-sharp.

"Ah, of course. Silly me. But you knew him?"

"Yeah, from the year before," James said.

"This was our second visit to Santa's pad, you see, Jass. Did I mention we met Santa? Twice, in fact!"

"Yes, you did. And I noted that."

James noticed the warmth leak from Jess's smile at Bear. Bear still had that way about him. Sure, people thought him a bit weird at first, but he soon charmed them and made them his best friend.

"So what happened the first time?" Jess asked

"Erm, we don't need to talk about that."

"James doesn't want to talk about that since that's the time he got us lost in the forest ... I told you we should've used the map!" Bear chided him.

"If only you were holding it the right way up!"

Bear chuckled a little before it turned into a cough. "Well, that's true."

"Not to mention you drew it," James added, beaming.

"Yes, I did, didn't I! I forgot that."

"So ..." prompted Jess.

James brushed a crumb off his jeans. "Let's just say it was the days before GPS. Some screaming, running, chasing, elves, and reindeer were involved."

Bear nodded. "The usual kind of stuff, eh, James?"

He grinned. "Yeah, the usual kind of stuff."

And it sort of was "usual" back then, James mused. Back before jobs and money (or the lack of) and designs and computers and banks.

"Okay, I'll admit I'm intrigued," Jess said. So Grenley—"

"*Grin*ley," Bear corrected her.

"Grinley said you had to save Christmas ..."

"Yep!" Bear said. "We might need some more tea ..."

Then

Bear

It had already started. The disorientation that preceded the journey. Hayley moved away—she was too young to come back then.

"Quick!" James said. "Coats!" He rushed into the hallway, and I followed.

We grabbed our coats and scarves and staggered back to the tree, where the effect was generated. I plumped down onto the floor and yanked my boots on—even bears need warmth against the snow, you see ... Well, not polar bears, obviously.

Anyway, James had his gear on, so he yanked me up. We both staggered as the spinning around us began. The tree was quickly a blur. At least we knew what to expect this time. You know, spinning and blurring and stuff.

And then we were there! I dunno why it again made us about a paw or three off the ground. But, as usual, we collapsed and felt something cold and wet on our faces. Well, James did first.

"Snow!" he cried. "Though I like it more when I'm standing."

I jumped up and splashed the fluffy snow with my boots. "The magic worked again!"

I looked around: as far as I could see, snow lay all around, deep and crisp and even. A gentle wind blew little snowflakes into our faces.

"Looks like we're back," James said.

"Yeah. Let's try not to get lost this time?"

"Did you bring a map?"

"No."

"Good. We should be fine then."

"You're funny, James. Not." He smiled. "Which way?"

"That way." James pointed. "Look, I can see smoke coming out of Santa's chimney, far away over there."

Off we went, trudging through the snow. When I looked back I could soon see our footprints stretching out, leaving a long line behind us. And further back, the tall, green trees of the forest with their white snow-covered tops were fading into the distance. I shivered, remembering what it was like being lost in there.

After a while, our heads covered in snowflakes, we arrived at Santa's house.

Strange, I thought. "It's very quiet inside, isn't it?"

"Mmm," James agreed. He went up to the front door. "It's open a little."

Together, we pushed it open a little more, enough to peer inside. To our amazement we saw ... nothing. And nobody. The huge table, where last year all the elves were busily making and wrapping presents, was empty. No elves and no presents—not a thing, not a soul.

I took my hat off and scratched my head. "Where is everyone?"

"Only one way to find out. Come on ..."

So in we went, closing the door and the cold weather behind us. We loosened our scarves and looked around. Nothing stirred on this night before Christmas. Not even a mouse.

So we walked to the end of the big room, towards where we remembered Santa's rooms were, James leading the way. He was always good like that. Always leading, always looking after me.

He yanked open the first door, and we peeked inside. And there we saw the giant Christmas tree. How sad he looked. But why?

"Hello," said James looking up at the tree.

Nothing. I'm not sure what I expected. I mean, I thought the tree spoke with us last time. I distinctly recall a whole convo with him … Or was that Santa. Probably Grinley, I s'pose.

"Santa hangs out in there, if I recall," James said. "Let's go on through, shall we?"

James knocked on the door of Santa's room. You could tell it was his room because it was wood. And in an arch shape. And it said "Santa" on it.

"Yes, come in!" sounded a voice.

We pushed open the door and stepped inside. At the side of the room, next to the fireplace with its warming, glowing, crackling orange fire, sat an old man with a white, bushy beard, dressed in red with black boots.

"Well, well, look who it is," Santa said, smiling. "Why, if it's not my little friends, James and Bear. Come in, come in."

We did, unwrapping our scarves as we neared the fireplace.

"No elves about, Santa?" James asked.

"And where are all the Christmas presents?" I added. Because, you know, presents are important, right?

"Oh … well …" Santa replied. Yes … deary, deary me. It happened last night, while we were all sleeping. They came and stole all the Christmas presents!"

"Gosh, *all* of the presents?" I asked. "Even ours?" Well, back in those days … I mean, you know, *presents. Christmas.*

"Yes, every last one of them. And now there'll be no presents for all the children this Christmas. It's a disaster!"

"Who took them?" James asked. Which was a good question, I thought because whoever it was, I wanted a word with them.

Just then, Grinley came into the room, carrying a small pile of wood in his arms, which he lay down by the side of the glowing log fire. "Those dastardly gnomes stole them alls! If I be a gettin' me 'ands on 'em, I'll be a showin' thems a thing or twos!"

He brushed the dirt from the wood off his hands onto his apron.

I know what you're wondering. What were gnomes doing at the North Pole? Isn't it just supposed to be elves and reindeer?

Well, that's what we thought. Although we were soon to discover there was worse. Much worse.

Now

Jess

"Can I stop you there?" Jess asked. "Sorry to interrupt. But I need some details, you see. Can you tell me about how the presents come to be, how so many are produced, and where?"

"Sure!" the bear said. "You tell her, James."

"Erm, well, not really. Sorry. I mean, as far as we knew, they worked all year round. The last time we were there, they were basically finishing off the wrapping on the big table."

"And eating Christmas pies, James!"

"Don't remind me!" James laughed. "I nearly barfed up from so many."

"Lightweight! He couldn't even manage a fifth one."

"I've hardly touched a Christmas-themed pastry since then!"

Jess sighed inwardly. James's mood had lightened considerably, and that was nice to see. But with a lack of detail, how would readers believe any of this ... this crazy story?

"Right, okay. Let's maybe work that out later."

"Yes, let's. Because there's worse to come. Much worse ..."

The bear's attempts to imitate a doomed-filled voice didn't really come off. His voice was a little croaky, although Jess noticed it—and he—perked up quite a lot telling the story.

"Much worse to come?"

"Yes."

"How so?"

"What lived in the mountain."

Then

James

♦ ♦ ♦

I asked Grinley about the gnomes. Turns out they were basically elves that went on strike and didn't get their wage demands met. They'd asked for fifty percent and Christmas off. Obviously that wasn't going to work. They'd gone down to Greenland to live in a mountain. You know, as you do.

"They's gottened bored or some such," Grinley said. "Bored so theys be comin' back and stealin' alls the presents!!"

I wondered how a bunch of gnomes could turn up from Greenland—obviously none too near—and grab a gazillion gifts. They must have had help, I reckoned. Like U-Haul or some such, maybe.

"I have an idea!" Bear cried. "Let's send out all the reindeer to find the gnomes and presents."

Bless him, Bear had loads of ideas back in the day. Just usually not very good ones. But this one ...

Santa sighed. "I already sent out the reindeer. This morning. They haven't returned—none of them! So now I've lost all my reindeer as well! It's a complete *disaster*. I'll just have to cancel Christmas this year."

"C-cancel Christmas?!" Bear sputtered. "But not yummy Christmas lunch, surely!"

"Unless ..."

"Unless what, Santa?" I said. I won't deny I was hoping he'd thought of something. I mean, who wants to lose their Christmas presents? And I'd never hear the end of it from Bear.

"Unless you two can help."

"No problem, Santa sir!" Bear even saluted, ever keen. And clearly motivated today. "At your service! We'll ... we'll ..."

"Balloons," I said.

"That's right," Bear agreed. "We'll balloons ... What?"

"You've got hot-air balloons, haven't you, Santa?" I recalled.

Santa nodded thoughtfully. "Hmm, a couple, yes. In the old stables. Haven't had them out for a while."

"I dunnos. Theys might've gotten a tear in 'em p'raps," Grinley said.

Santa put on his hat and Grinley took off his apron—I remember he was quite fastidious about not wearing his "inside" apron outside—and we all left Santa's Grotto.

This was more like it—a plan and some positivity! Those were the days. Before plans involved rent and budgets.

"It be right good yous is 'ere," Grinley said to me. "What with Santa n mees none toos young and the elves never 'avin' much in the way of long eyesight. What with all theirs focus on makin' stuff and wrappin' stuff, we normally would bees relyin' on the reindeers. But yous young 'uns'll be able to sees stuff."

Now
Jess

"We trotted outside again, to the stables and found the balloons," James said.

"Mm. The baskets weren't too big though, but big enough for a crew of three."

"Crew ...?" Jess asked.

The bear coughed a couple of times.

"Alright, mate?" his old friend asked him.

Jess watched James pat the bear on the back, helping him to sip some water.

"Thanks, James. Now, um what was I saying? Presents ...?"

"The crew for the balloon."

"He means the two elves plus each of us," James said.

"Yep, one elf to fly the thing and um, one to stand on so James and I could see. We ... weren't as big back then."

"Some of us still aren't," James ribbed.

"And some of us grew out as well as up!"

Jess noted the warmth of their smiles at each other. No log fire was needed in here today.

"How did you fill the balloons?" she asked.

"Propane," James said.

"Pro-pain? That's one of my pills, I think. Sounds like it. There are so many these days."

"The tanks of propane, remember?"

"There were tanks? Like, toy ones ...? Eh? Don't recall those."

Jess smiled. "So you filled up the balloons with hot air using the propane and ..."

"Yeah. Well, the elves did," James said.

"They're jolly handy to have around, you know, elves," the bear said.

"Yeah, a bunch of the elves dragged the balloons outside and filled them. Didn't have to wait too long. There was sort of bad news, though, with the plan."

"Oh, what?"

"One-way trip," the bear said.

"How come?"

"Unless we could locate the reindeer to fly back on, we'd be stuck," James told her. "At least until they could get back with the balloons."

"The fuel. Yes, of course—it doesn't last that long. The balloons couldn't hang around, as it were, for too long, right?"

"Right. And certainly not land and take off again. Plus there was only limited fuel in the stables back at The Pole. They'd have to locate more canisters before they could get back to us."

"So why two balloons? Why not one?"

"Grinley was right," the bear said. "There were slight tears in the fabric of both."

"We had to take both—each as backup for the other."

"Ergo, a one-way balloon trip," the bear added.

Jess nodded as she jotted notes down on her notepad. "You'd have thought Santa would have more reliable backup transport."

"You'd think. Bear mentioned that."

"But when Santa smiles, what's a bear to do? In for a penny and all that."

James smiled at his friend. "Always the way, eh, Bear?

"'Twas always thus, James. 'Twas always thus."

"Anyway, before long, we were up and away."

"Flying in a balloon! I've always wanted to do that," Jess said. "Sounds like fun."

The bear coughed a little and James patted him.

"Fun? Well, not at first ..."

Then
Bear

The basket lurched, and I grabbed hold of something. Turned out to be an elf's hat. I stumbled a bit, but the basket saved me from tumbling out. I s'pose falling on my bottom was the better option. How on earth had James and I found ourselves at the North Pole (with no Christmas!), my rump sliding across a basket in a chilly balloon bound for Greenland?

I could hear the basket drag slightly across the snow, and then ... suddenly it was ... *calm*. As calm as a kitten falling asleep in a bear's lap.

So ... gentle.

The pirate elf, I can't remember his name, pulled on a cord, and the whoosh of flames rushed up, creating the lift.

My copirate elf was Grinley. I was a bit worried about him being so old and whatnot, but his job was to balance me on his shoulders if they needed help navigating.

"Up you goes, Bear. 'S alright. Ol' Grinley can still er, *bear*, ha-ha, some weight."

He bent down, and I clambered onto his shoulders. He rose, slowly and steadily—like some kind of weightlifter at the Olympics—and wow! I could see we were *flying*!

And there was James, on an elf's shoulders, just like me.

"James!" I cried, waving frantically at him. There weren't too many feet between us, but the roar of the flames on the gas drowned my voice out quite a lot. Even though I had a bit of a roar myself in those days.

"Alright, Bear?!" James shouted back. "This is a bit fun, eh?"

"Not bad, eh! You know 'Adventure' is my middle name!"

Back at school, they called me "Adventure Bear," you see.

The wind blew strongly in our faces, and our scarves flapped away as we began our journey down to Greenland. Although it was only about an hour, I'd hoped there might be some service on board—just a cuppa and some cake or something. Even a flask of tea and a prepacked slice would have been fine. I'm easy to please, you see. But no deal. Still, it was quite cool to watch the pirate elf engage the turbo thingies to really propel us.

Anyway, after a while, I could feel we were descending, and Grinley let me pop my head up again. It was good to see James's balloon flying right alongside us.

A few more minutes and we touched down.

Greenland ... It looked just like the North Pole, I thought. Snow everywhere. Except for the mountain next to us, that is.

I looked up at the huge crag, all the way to its peak. Well, I assumed the peak. It disappeared into the low clouds.

"That's where theys lives," Grinley said, jumping out of the basket. "Thems naughty gnomes live in a dark cave in that mountain ... I beens 'ere once."

"I think I see an opening," James said, coming over to us. "Over there on the left."

"'S about right, if I recalls."

"Time for a reccy, I reckon. Bear?"

"I s'pose," I said. I mean it was all very well being Adventure Bear and everything but a cup of tea and a slice really wouldn't have gone amiss before we set off for the mountain. Maybe the gnomes had tea inside? Probably not. Still in for a penny, in for a pound (of cake, I hoped).

Grinley volunteered to stay behind. "My bones're too olds now to be trudgin' up rocks 'n' things," he said. "That's why you young uns're 'ere."

I thought he was skipping out on the hard work. Of course, now, I understand about bones and old ... (I wonder what happened to old Grinley?)

"Heres," he said, holding out two tubes about the size of long slim drinking glasses. I like my milk in those—always have done.

I tapped the one he handed me—claws are good for tapping on things, you see. Hmm, plastic, not glass. That was good. Inside was purple glitter, stuffed solid, it looked like.

"What is this?" I asked the old elf.

"It be hows yous'll get the presents back. We uses this glitter-dustin' to loads the sleigh. Wees developed it 'bout 'undred years agos. It don' 'alf make the loadins easier!"

"How does it work?" James asked.

"Simples. Yous just be pressin' the bottom to activates it. Give it abouts ten seconds, point it at the presents, 'n' press the bottoms agains. The glitter-dustin's'll doos the rest."

"Couldn't we use it on ourselves?" I asked. "To get back too, I mean."

"Alas not, my lil friend. It don't be workin' on peoples, see. Nor bears."

James nodded.

"I bees right sorry we can'ts bees 'ere to take yous back."

"It's alright, Grinley. A plan is a plan, eh, Bear?

"I s'pose."

"We'll be fine. And we'll find the reindeer, I'm sure. And Adventure Bear here is definitely motivated to get his Christmas presents back. Right, mate?"

"You've got a point, James. Motivation is the key. Tea, too, of course."

"Well, good lucks to yous both. Yous be our last chances for Christmas. So long."

As Grinley turned back to the balloons, we put the tubes inside our coat pockets and buttoned up again against the cold.

"Ready, Bear?"

I nodded, giving James a thumbs-up. (Sort of part paw with claw.) "I'm 'Ready Bear.'"

We set off to find the entrance. The elves had put us down quite close, so we weren't too far away, luckily.

"There," James said, pointing to an opening in the mountain. "A cave. And there's a sign above, I think."

We walked up and, yes, just above the entrance to the cave, there was a sign, which read: "NAUGHTY GNOME CAVE."

But it was when I read the sign underneath that made me sure we wouldn't find any cake inside. Or tea.

Now

James

"Bear, you didn't seriously expect to find tea inside the gnomes' cave, did you?"

"Well, no. Not really. Maybe some cake in a packet or something, though."

James smiled. "I don't remember you being so optimistic, mate!"

"Mm, back at school, they used to call me that: 'Optimistic Bear.'"

"I thought you were 'Adventure Bear,'" Jess said, finishing her tea.

"Erm, yes, that too, erm ... Jazz."

"Jess."

Bear nodded and coughed, a cough that shook his little frame, and James, already sitting beside him, held him to try to absorb some of the vibrations wracking his friend.

"Alright?"

"I-I ... yes, I will be, thanks. Good days and bad days ... Though they're getting worse, these coughs."

"Want some more tea?"

"No ... no, thanks. I just need to rest here a moment. Catch my breath ... May I get that little blanket ...? Oh, thank you. Just tuck it in there around my legs, if you would. Thank you ... You tell her the story, James."

James looked up at Jess and noted the concern on her face. That was nice. He was glad it had been her that answered the phone.

"So, tell me, what was on the sign," she said.

"Oh, just something about a dragon."

"A *dragon*? What dragon?"

Then

James

🔔 🔔 🔔

"D-d-dragon? What d-dragon?" Bear gulped. "You didn't say anything about a d-dragon!"

I read the second sign: "KEEP OUT! ALL VISITORS WILL BE COOKED AND EATEN BY THE DRAGON." I didn't think much of the typography or font choice. A bit dull, I thought. A serif face would have been much better.

"Probably just wrote that to scare people," I said. "I see it worked, Adventure Bear."

Bear straightened himself. "No, no, absolutely not ...! D-dragons don't bother me, you know! Back at school, they actually call me 'Danger Bear'!"

I just smiled. "Well, come on then, Danger Bear, and let's see what's inside."

"Um, it does look rather dark ... No problem—none at all."

"Good. Come on then, DB!"

I didn't have to duck much to get in—Bear of course didn't. But he was right: it was pretty dark. And cold too. He shivered—just from the cold, of course—and sniffed the dirty-smelling air.

But the good news was that after a minute, it wasn't so dark. Flame torches lined the wall down into the cave. Their flickering light caused shadows to dance on the rocks. I don't know if Bear noticed how the shapes were kind of scary at first, but I didn't want to make him any more nervous.

We walked on, sometimes stumbling slightly on stones that were lying in wait, basically invisible on the ground. Like my Lego used to be at home.

"I wonder how far in we'll need to go," Bear said. "Maybe—"

Suddenly there was a low rumbling and moaning sound from deep inside the mountain.

Bear gasped. "D-d-dragon!"

We stood, frozen like ice statues in the wavering torchlight, afraid to move. But the rumbling sound didn't come again.

"Come on," I said. We continued on for another minute before I noticed something. "I think I can see a little red light in the distance." Slowly we moved towards it. "Is it me or is the light moving?"

"Is it me or is it moving towards *us*?

"It is."

We stopped. The light continued to approach.

"Wait, it's—"

"Rudolph!" Bear exclaimed.

"Bear?" Rudolph said. "Is that you?"

"Yes!"

"Are you alright?" Bear asked the reindeer. "What happened to you and the reindeer squad?"

"Yes, well, sorry about this, but the gnomes caught us in a big net. They must have figured we were coming."

"But how did they get you all?" I asked.

"Yes, that is a valid question."

"And the answer is ...?"

"Well, you know how we like to fly in formation. *Bam!* We were all in the net together."

"Ah, I see."

"Yes, um, we'll do better next time," he said, clearly a bit embarrassed. "They quickly collapsed the net around us and we were caught like flies in a web. Though with much less room, all lumped together as we were. Then they dumped us in a cave room down there. We've been digging as best we can. I finally managed to wriggle my way out from under the door."

"Good. Well done, Rudy. We'll get you all out. But we need to know—"

"About the presents! Where are the Christmas presents?" Bear demanded. "And the d-dragon?"

"The presents are all sitting in the huge cave, where those horrid gnomes sleep. They didn't even open them yet."

"Well, that's a relief," Bear said.

"But we'll need some glitter-dusting to get them out."

"No probs—we brought the dusty stuff—but what about the *d-dragon*?!"

Rudolph twitched an ear. "The der-dragon ...? Oh! There's no dragon. The gnomes just put that sign there to scare people away."

"Exactly. That's what I told Danger Bear here."

"*Danger* Bear?"

"Don't ask," I said.

"I don't mind danger ... I just don't fancy the idea of being chased by a der-dragon, I mean a d-dragon, thank you."

"Although ..."

Bear caught my look. "Although what? There's no der-dragon and there's no *although*."

"So what was that rumbling sound, then?"

"Um ..."

"Probably just an echo in the caves," Rudolph said. "We hear it sometimes. Don't worry. I was about to free us all—the silly gnomes left the key in the door—when I heard your voices and came to investigate."

"Yes, let's get you all out before—"

"The der-dragon that definitely doesn't exist turns up," Bear said.

"Before we locate the presents," I said.

"OK. This way to the reindeer, guys."

Rudolph led us further into the cave, where a few yards down, there was a huge fork.

"That's where the gnomes live," Rudolph said. "As best we understand from the noise down there. They watch movies, I think. They seem to like James Bond."

We took the left fork, which led us to the cave room with the reindeer. The door looked heavy. But Rudy was righty—the key was in the door, the lock, though, oddly high up.

"You want to do the honors, Bear?"

"Don't mind if I do! Give me a lift up."

I bent down and made a cradle with my hands to give Bear a platform. I lifted him so he could reach the key, which he turned easily. He jumped down and dusted off his paws.

"Job well done, Bear."

"Why, thank you, James. I learned how to pick locks in school, you know."

"Of course you did."

I pulled on the heavy wooden door, slowly dragging it open. The reindeer all rose and bustled as we entered.

"Folks," Bear announced, "prebear to be rescued! This is a bear's bust-out!"

I chuckled. Quickly, I led us all down the cave, urging silence. When we got to the end, we agreed on a plan. Rudolph, Bear, and I would sneak into the gnomes' cave and locate the presents.

"There aren't too many gnomes guarding them," Rudolph informed us. "They live on the other side of the mountain mainly."

"So, we need to tempt them out." I looked at Bear and his little legs. "That's down to you, I think, Rudy. You'll be able to escape before they get to you."

"And we'll do the business with the present dusting," Bear said. "Yes! I like my bit in this plan. No gnome- or der-dragon-tangling for me!"

"For any of us, I hope," I added. "Come on then."

We made our way back into the cave. Rudolph's nose helped out, bathing the area in front of us in a pale-red light. We turned down the right fork, slowing as we heard noises and saw light at the end.

There was no door to their cave, but the entrance was huge—obviously why they'd chosen this place to keep their loot.

"You ready, Rudes?" I whispered to the reindeer.

He didn't answer immediately. I figured he wasn't looking forward to facing them again, having tangled with—and been entangled by—them before.

"It's a good plan, don't worry," Bear said. "You'll speed down the tunnel and launch into the air, no worries."

Rudolph nodded. "OK, ready."

I nodded to him, and Bear and I positioned ourselves either side of the entrance, our backs firmly pressed against the cold rock. I nodded at Rudy again, and he snorted before prancing right into the room.

"Good evening, gentlegnomes! Got a bit bored next door. The hay really isn't that good, and don't even *talk* to me about the room service! And, you know, been aching for a bit of exercise. Anyone up for a chase scene ...? Oh, you are! Great ... I'll just turn around and ..."

The reindeer shot out of the entrance with a "Byeeeeeeeeeeee!"

A beat ... and then out shot a bunch of gnomes, too many of them to count, shouting and screeching and chasing after the reindeer. The gnomes were nothing if not predictable.

"Let's do this!" I hissed at Bear, and we dashed inside.

On the walls, flame torches lit the cave, bathing it in a warm glow. The cave was divided into two. On the right was, I guess, their living area. Which was kind of like a home theater. There was a huge screen with about twenty or so seats in front of it, and it was silently playing something ... Penguins were skating on ice. Must be the locals, I thought. Ah, no ... The green frog decked in Victorian garb could only mean one thing: "The Muppet Christmas Carol." (At least the gnomes had good taste.)

"I reckon you could have been in that," I said to Bear.

"Yes! Like 'The Ghost of Christmas Presents' or something?"

"Ha! Good one, mate. Talking of Christmas presents ..."

"Mm ... Look, James. There's an opening over there."

We made our way past some kind of kitchen/dining area on the other side of the cave. It was strewn with dirty goblets and metal plates, and even Bear turned his nose up the mess (and that didn't happen often) as we walked past. The entrance broke left again after a few feet, and Bear gasped.

Here, in this storage cave, lay the gazillion gifts. All still wrapped in beautifully designed paper of all colors and hues. Ribbons—red mainly—hugged themselves around some of the boxes. All present and correct.

"This is ... it's ..." Bear began.

"Amazing. I know!"

"I wonder where ours are."

Well, of course Bear would wonder that.

"Let's not look now, eh? Once the gnomes work out they won't be able to catch Rudy & the gang again, they'll be back here pretty quick."

Bear gave me that look, and I knew what was coming.

"I guess they have, erm, *gnome*where else to go!"

"Really? Now, mate?"

"Come on, that was good!"

"You want to be here and tell it to them when they get back?"

"Gnome way."

"Oh, stop it!"

"Sorry. But you're right: there is definitely, erm, 'clear and present danger.'"

I sighed. His jokes usually came in threes. "Come on—the glitter-dusting. Let's get this pile of presents back to where they're supposed to be. Santa & the sleigh gang will need to be off before long."

We took our tubes out from our coats.

"Now we're here and there's this huge pile of yummy presents, these tubes do seem pretty small," Bear said.

"Yeah. Hope there's enough of this stuff inside."

We placed ourselves about thirty feet apart from one another. Bear planted his paw feet firmly apart, like some cool cop would on the firing range, his tube gripped firmly in both paw hands.

"So, we first push the bottom once to activate it and then again to launch the dusting. Ready, Bear?"

"I was born ready."

"You certainly were, Cliché Bear."

"I'm not kitschy!"

I smiled to myself. "Activate on three. Three, two, one—*activate*."

We pressed up on the bottom of the tubes.

"Mine's vibrating a little."

"Mine too," I said. "Ready to fire?"

"Yeah. We gotta save Christmas—gotta do it for the kids. Let's do this."

I rolled my eyes. "Three, two, one—*fire!*"

Simultaneously, we depressed the tubes, and a with a solid-sounding *pop!* they burst open. Glittery dust shot out and ... hung there in front of us.

"Huh?" I mumbled.

The glitter floated, suspended, shimmering in the flickering torchlight of the cave. As I watched, the clouds expanded in size and the glitter particles danced around, frantic, as if not knowing what to do.

If they didn't know, we certainly didn't.

Bear looked at me. "Shouldn't it be—?"

Suddenly, the clouds surged towards the mountain of presents. With a distinct tingling sound, particles sprinkled onto the bottom of the mound and began to work their way upwards.

"Look!" Bear cried. "They're disappearing!"

Bear was right! As the glitter-dusting made its way up the pile, we could see the cave wall beyond. Within seconds, there was just half the pile of presents left, now suspended in the air. And then they were all gone! The glitter-dusting too.

"That's—"

"Amazing!" Bear said for the both of us.

We looked at each other and smiled. Another job well done.

"We came and we kicked it into touch, baby!"

"We did!" I agreed.

"Time we hightail it outta here, James. Back at The Pole, there's a flask of hot tea with my name on it ..."

"No arguments here."

We rushed out of the big cave, up the tunnel, and out into the daylight.

"So good to breathe fresh air again!" Bear said. "What the ...?"

Oh-oh! A crowd of gnomes was running towards us, shouting and screeching. Flying reindeer were swooping and laughing, getting their revenge on the nasty little creatures. Well, it did serve them right. Except they were now headed for us—with renewed vigor, it looked like!

A brown form swooped down from above us.

"Rudy!" I cried as he landed. "Nice one, mate."

"Here comes Miss Piggy, too."

Had I heard that right? "Miss Piggy?"

"I know! She's one of the young ones we're training."

"I guess pigs do fly then."

"Seems so. Quickly now! James, jump onto me. I need to take the heavier of you guys."

I wanted Bear on board and away first, but there was no time to argue. Rudolph bent down and I jumped on just as the other reindeer, Miss Piggy, landed. Bear took a few paces back and ran and jumped too, grabbing onto her fur. She rose and sprang.

Bear yelped.

"I gots one!" a gnome shouted.

"Bear!" I cried as he began to rise into the air.

"Argh!" Bear squealed.

"Bear!" I watched as Miss Piggy rose, the gnome hanging on for dear life. She dived down and skimmed the ground. You almost had to feel sorry for the gnome as his feet smacked onto the ground and were dragged across it. His yelping and squealing didn't last—he soon let go—and Miss Piggy climbed back up into the sky triumphantly.

"Don't mess with us brown furs, buddy!" Bear cried as they flew up.

High into the sky we all flew while down on the ground, the gnomes were shouting and shaking their fists angrily.

"Ha-ha!" Bear laughed. "No Christmas presents for them!"

We were home-free.

I thought.

That was when we heard it ... a huge rumbling sound coming from the mountain, and suddenly, the side of the mountain exploded, spraying rocks out into the air! Stones and shards showered all around us, temporarily blinding the reindeer. They both halted mid-air.

As the view cleared, I saw a massive, monstrous creature burst out of the hole in the mountain. Flames burst from its mouth.

"D-d-dragon!!" Bear cried.

Now
James

🔔 🔔 🔔

"What?" Jess said, fully into the events now, James saw.

"Yep, fire in the hole! It was real ..." Bear coughed, and James wrapped the blanket a little more snugly around him. "I knew it! We never got away that easy, did we, James?"

James nodded and smiled. "No, mate. Not usually ... Are you warm enough?"

"You know, maybe I'd like to pop back into bed now. Stretch out these old bones a little."

"Sure. I'll give you a hand."

Jess got up too and went to the bed to turn down the covers as James helped his friend down.

"Thanks, Jess," James said.

"Of course."

James helped Bear into bed. He felt so frail in his arms. Jess fussed over Bear while James poured some water on the little table beside the bed.

"Oh, thank you ... Jazz, isn't it?"

"It's Jess," she gently reminded him.

"Jess. Yes. That rhymes, you know."

Jess smiled. "I guess it does. So, this dragon then ..."

"Oh, don't worry about a little old dragon. Danger Bear could always deal with them! Well, not the fiery breath so much. Bears have fur, you see. Easily singed. Here, look ..." Bear showed her the back of one of his arms. "This patch never quite grew back the same."

James knew about the fur, of course. He watched Jess lean in.

"Oh. Nasty." She scribbled a note onto her pad. "The dragon ... I suppose it was green. They always draw them greenish, don't they?"

"Not green, no ..." Bear said.

"Red," James said.

Then

James

A dark, crimson red, with ugly green veins in its immense wings, the dragon screeched and screamed, with fire and smoke shooting out from its mouth and nose as it flapped its enormous wings. And seated on its back was a furious-looking gnome.

The gnome shouted something to the dragon, who gave an angry, fiery roar. It flapped its wings and made for us.

"Reindeer! We. Are. *Leaving!*" Rudolph shouted. "Fasten your seatbelt, James, and be sure to hang on."

I looked over at Bear and Miss Piggy. He had both paws gripped onto the young reindeer's neck. He gave me a quick thumbs-up. The reindeer squad formed up and, with Rudolph in front, together we shot off, gathering speed with every second.

I looked over my shoulder and gulped as I saw the giant der-dragon—the dragon—was already almost upon us. It spat flames, singeing one of the reindeer.

"Break, break, *break*!" shouted Rudolph over his shoulder. "Give it more targets! It's got us for top speed—evasive pattern 'Sleigh *Five*'!" He snorted. "James, you good?"

"I'm good."

"Then hang on!"

My stomach lurched as my ride banked left and dropped several feet in an instant. I felt our speed decrease as I was pressed into Rudolph's neck.

The dragon shot forward in front of us but suddenly shaped its wings like a sail to dramatically slow its momentum. Unbelievably, it made a summersault three-sixty and made right at us once more. I couldn't help but notice its design was pretty effective. I'd have to get sketching one day.

The reindeer swooped and dived, avoiding the flames shooting out at them. Poor Bear just clung onto Miss Piggy, his little arms wrapped around her neck, hanging on as tightly as he could!

Annoyed and spurred on by the gnome, the dragon roared and screeched even louder and tried to swat us with its wings. But the reindeer were too agile.

The dragon flew around, faster and faster, bellowing fire, flapping and swiping with its wings. Around and around the mountain it chased us. The reindeer dived downwards and swooped upwards— anything to avoid the dragon's fire and claws!

Down below, the gnomes cheered and screamed encouragement at the dragon.

"Look out!" I shouted into the wind. "Beeeaaaar!"

The beast was making for Bear and Miss Piggy. And it was almost on top of them. Fire leaped from the dragon's mouth, licking both sets of fur.

Miss Piggy flew upwards, as fast as anything, but still she could not shake off the dreadful creature snorting at her tail. It unfurled its terrible, sharp claws to grab her. If only Bear had been on Rudolph or another of the more experienced reindeer, I thought.

Miss Piggy banked right, banked left, and the dragon's claws missed her rump by inches. It roared and spat flames, but Miss Piggy had anticipated that and dropped a few feet below. The flames passed harmlessly above.

She slowed a little, it seemed, looked over her shoulder, and ... winked!

What?

The dragon roared, the veins in its neck pulsating in fury.

"Come on, Scaley!" Miss Piggy taunted it. "If you're tough enough!" She swished her tail in mockery and plunged.

"Aaaargh!" Bear cried out.

That dragon roared flames out, bent its long neck down, and it, too, plunged in chase.

"Hang on, James," Rudolph said to me. "I know what she's doing. But we better follow just in case."

Two reindeer, a dragon, a gnome, a bear, and a human (you know, as you get) flew down from the sky. Down and down, heading straight for the bottom of the mountain, flew Miss Piggy—as fast as an arrow. So fast she must surely crash.

Huddled into Miss Piggy's neck, Bear couldn't resist a look behind. He screamed as the dragon closed.

"Bear!" I gasped as they were brief seconds from the ground and impact.

The dragon stretched its claws and swiped at the reindeer, tearing a red whelp in her rump.

It roared in its success.

Which is why it realized its fate too late.

In a gravity-defying move, Miss Piggy leveled off, her hooves scratching across the ground, and stretched her neck to breaking point to regain height.

The dragon wasn't as agile ... It slammed into the ground and rolled over and over, its screeches of pain and anger piercing my ears. Rudolph's twitched, too. The gnome was sent flying ... somewhere. We never saw him again. Finally, the beast came to a skidding halt.

Rudolph flew us over to Miss Piggy.

"Nice erm, piloting, Bear," I said. He looked at me groggily and raised a bear thumbs-up.

"Miss Piggy, that was ... nice flying," Rudolph said.

"Pah! I've done that in training loads of times."

"Really?"

"Well, in the simulator. But, darn, it was a blast, eh, Bear?"

Still woozy, Bear looked at me and muttered, "Yeah, fun. Sure ... What ...?" His eyes suddenly focused and his mouth dropped open. "Look! The d-dragon—it's getting up again!"

Sure enough, the dragon was rising shakily into the air. It shook its head, flapped its wings, and began to climb. Only now, its wings beat less powerfully and less in time. The beast flew dizzily, like it'd had one too many.

It tried to breathe heat, but its fire had gone out. In more ways than one, evidently, as the dragon decided it'd had enough and turned around, disappearing off around the side of the mountain.

Now

Jess

"That's quite the story," Jess said.

"Yes, I guess it is," James replied. "But it happened, just as we told it. Pretty much, anyway. I mean, it's been a few years."

James looked at her. His face told her she needed to believe it. As is.

And finally, she got it. Understood why she was here.

"Yes, yes, it all happened, alright," Bear said. "My memory's pin-sharp, Jazz. Besides, if we've made it up, there would have been ... um ... been a lot more tea involved!"

Jess nodded and smiled. "And cake, Bear?"

"Mmm, yes." Bear sighed and began another fit of coughing.

A care assistant entered the room to administer some medicine to Bear. Jess thought she caught a sad look at James. Perhaps a very slight shake of her head? James looked away.

When she left, Jess regarded the little old bear, his fur grayed, stubbled, and matted. What a strange friend for James to have shared childhood adventures with. Had they really met Santa and saved Christmas? It seemed like a fantasy, a dream one of them had had. Except, she realized, their story did sync perfectly as they told it. And there had been references to other adventures, she'd noted.

Did it matter, though? Whether things happened as they said. No, she realized. That was their story, but her story for the paper was about the here and now: about shared times and the bonds that are never broken. Well, only broken ultimately. It seemed the little bear's adventures were almost at their end.

This, she realized, was his epilogue.

"Tell me," she began, shaking herself back into the here and now. "Was Christmas saved then?"

"Mm? Christmas ...? Oh, yes, Christmas ... We saved Christmas once, Jazz. Did you know?"

James nodded, but his heart looked broken.

"Yeah, it was saved. Bear saved Christmas. Didn't you, mate?"

"Mmm, I did ... And you helped, too, James ... I never could have done it without you." Bear's breathing had become more labored.

"No, Bear. *I* never would have done any of it without *you*."

James wiped a tear from his eye.

Jess waited a moment. "You both got back home from the North Pole ..."

"Yeah," James said, composing himself. "A chilly flight back on the reindeer. Santa and Grinley were there, of course, and were happy to see us. They'd already loaded up the sleigh. And batches of presents were laid out, ready for the glitter-dusting to transport them onto the sleigh as each batch got delivered."

"We rode on Santa's ... sleigh, Jazz," Bear croaked. "Did you know that?"

"That's amazing, Bear," Jess said. "And after you'd saved Christmas!"

"Yes, that's right ... We did ... Can't remember when though."

Jess took Bear's paw in her hand. "The only thing that's important is you did what you did together as best friends."

"Friends ..." Bear wheezed. "James ... he's my best one."

Jess sniffed. She looked up at James. "I think I should leave you both now."

James nodded, swallowed. "Thanks for coming."

"It's ... been amazing. Really. To meet you both and hear about your adventure. Bear, I'll be leaving now. Thank you so much for the tea."

"Oh ... is there tea ...? Not for me ... Just had one. At The Pole ... I think it was." His breathing rasped. "James ...?"

"I'm here, mate," James said, stroking Bear's paw. "I'll always be here."

"I ... I'm sorry ... to leave you."

James's tears trickled down his cheek freely.

"'S alright, Bear. You'll feel better in the morning ... I know you will."

Bear rasped, "It's time ... I think. I'm ... all done in ... Sorry ..."

"No, Bear!"

"It was always ... fun, James ... Oh my ..."

And just like that, his breathing ceased and a sense of subdued peace was in the room.

Jess looked at the crestfallen man in front of her. He looked beyond disconsolate.

"I'm so sorry," she whispered. "I-I'll leave you alone."

James nodded. "Yeah," he croaked out.

Jess quickly gathered her coat and notepad and left the room with a small wave of acknowledgment, leaving James alone with his friend, together for the last time.

Their story had ended, but she would write it for others to share.

The end ...

The Bells of Christmas II

... Or maybe not ...

Now

Bear's eye popped open.

James jumped.

"She gone, James?"

"What the ...? Bear?"

"Mm?"

"I thought ... I thought ..."

"Oh, sorry. I get so sleepy sometimes. It's all those propane pills they give me, I think."

"But ... but ... you said about leaving me and stuff!"

"Oh, yes. Sorry. I thought it would make a neat ending for that lady's story. Nice lady that Jazz."

"It's Jess ... You ... you ..." James hugged Bear, squeezing him tightly.

"Easy, James. I'm not quite as young as I once was, you know."

"Sorry." James beamed at Bear, wiping his eyes a little.

"Come on then, help me out of bed."

"What?"

Bear pushed back on the covers and made to jump down. James instinctively gave him a helping hand.

"What are you doing?"

"Pass me my coat, will you? And scarf ... Come on!"

"No! I mean ... why? Where are you going?"

"Where are *we* going, James."

"Where are *we* going?" James said as he helped Bear into his coat. He donned his own and grabbed his beanie from his pocket.

Bear opened the door and peeked out. He turned back to James.

"All clear. Come on! We're busting out of this joint."

"You can't!"

"Yes, *we* can. Come on."

"Where?"

"There's an old radio, really old with vacuum tubes and stuff, that I found in a cupboard of junk."

"A radio ... So?"

"So ... it's a time machine! Come on, James, you really must keep up."

"But ..."

"Come on! I'm propane-fueled, remember? We're going. And that's my last word on the matter."

Bear strode—perhaps hobbled—out, leaving a flabbergasted James.

James smiled, stuffed his beanie back in his pocket, and followed his friend out the door.

"Where are we going?" he called out as Bear rounded a corner.

"To save the New Year, of course!"

Author's thanks

Thanks to Keith A. Pearson for allowing me to borrow his old radio time machine from his hugely fun novel *Tuned Out*. Perhaps Bear lives at the same care home. I highly recommend Keith's novel. Find it, among other places, at Amazon.

While some (☺) of the events in this story are fictionalized, this story features actual people. I began a series of James and Bear stories in the late 1990s for a very specific target readership. A readership of one: my nephew James. "Oh, the cleverness of me," to quote J.M. Barrie again. Well, of James: he had a brilliant imagination from a young age, was able to grasp concepts and create imagery in his mind. He would sometimes stare, transfixed, as I read to him. And for a few years, the first thing he'd ask me when I visited was whether I'd written him a new story. And how Bear was doing. ("Might have" and "We'll have to see" were always my answers, if you'd like to know.) Then, of course, one year, James didn't ask. He had "to go to school and learn solemn things," and his adventures with a little bear (sadly for his eternally lost boy uncle) *pawsed*, as it were. At least until now …

Thanks to James, Jess, Hayley (Nice-Niece … sorry your parts were cut), and Bear for allowing me to use their real names and to James and Bear for letting me feature a modified version of an actual adventure they shared one Christmas.

This story is to let James know that, after nearly a quarter of a century, Bear is doing just fine. He still loves supping on a cuppa and munching on cake (still chocolate mostly), recalling all their adventures together. The cake is in spite of his doctor's advice. But Bear insists cake is just fine, thank you very much. Which are, in fact, his last words on the matter.

Will Knight
Bio

Will Knight is the pseudonym for a micro-well-known copyeditor for award-winning and next-gen authors.

Di/Ary of Days, his first published entry using this pen name, appeared in Papillon du Père's anthology **13 by 11**.

Highly cultured, Will can be spotted out hunting for Christmas hamburgers, often spotting them in the snow and occasionally bagging a couple for tea. When not hunting and not editing or writing for other people, Will enjoys a game of Jenga—a game he equates with life: a steadily increasing challenge of balance ... and being prepared to start again.

He can be contacted care of the publisher, mail@papillon-du-pere.com.

THE SUGAR PLUM REDUX

LILLA GLASS

... Curtain ...
Entrées

Saliva dripped from the beast's fanged maw, matting its fur into stalactites as it stalked forward, hackles bristled and eyes glowing amber. It could not have looked more out-of-place, skulking through the toy-riddled bedroom, illuminated by the soft glow of a dinosaur-shaped nightlight. Come to think of it, Sugar Plum would have given her left wing to face off against a dinosaur. Even a little one. Werewolves had become straight-up blasé.

A dearth of imagination; that's what it is, she thought, debating whether to blame reality TV or understocked libraries. Perhaps, by now, there was a third societal malady to point the finger at—it was difficult to track the passage of time, relatively speaking.

The werewolf hadn't yet noticed her, though she'd announced herself with her signature spray of silvery sparkles. Neither had the cowering child in the corner—Eugene Kole, according to the logs. Sugar Plum tried her best not to take it personally, since both parties were otherwise occupied. In fact, that werewolf was well within pouncing distance of Eugene. Were it a *real* monster, it would have already devoured him. Thankfully, nightmares fed off suspense, not flesh.

Well, not *human* flesh.

Sugar Plum untied the shimmering satchel that hung from her gumdrop-studded belt, thinking back on simpler times, when her job had consisted of casually tossing candied fruits into the minds of restless dreamers before fluttering off to the next vision. Fruit, it seemed, was no longer a sufficient solution for life's slavering little woes.

Chocolate, however ...

Sugar Plum sorted through a week's worth of peppermints, caramel chews, and gummy bears until she found a sizable square of marbled fudge, wrapped in festive crimson cellophane. *Perfect!* She tossed the plastic wrap to the floor beside her, then gave a sharp, two-fingered whistle. "Here, boy!"

Both Eugene and the wolf turned bewildered eyes her way. The boy's widened on her glittery, gossamer wings; the beast's widened on the morsel in her fingers, already melting. With something between a growl and a whimper, the werewolf spun to fully face Sugar Plum, its pink tongue lolling out one side of its mouth.

"Who's a good boy?" she asked, shaking the treat.

The wolf's tail wagged an eager answer: *Me! I am! I'm a good boy!* Clearly, it was a dishonest appendage; if the werewolf were a good boy, Sugar Plum wouldn't have been summoned to slay it.

"Sit," Sugar Plum ordered, and the werewolf practically kowtowed. "Now, fetch." She tossed the fudge over her shoulder, and the wolf leapt after it. As it tore into the treat, Sugar Plum took the opportunity to approach young Mr. Eugene.

"A-are you a fairy?" the boy asked.

Sugar Plum rolled her eyes. "No, I'm the abominable snowman; hence the wings and tiara and stupid sugar-sprinkled skirt."

Eugene unfurled slowly, apparently unscathed by the sarcasm. "D-do you grant wishes?"

Wishes? Really? Oh, for Santa's sake! "Sure, I grant wishes, so long as that wish sounds something like, 'Please ma'am, can you slay the monster in my head so I can get some shuteye and you can get on with your job?' But if you're asking for a pony or a Red Ryder BB gun, you'll have to write the man up north and pray you've made the good list, because—"

The boy let out a startled yelp, folding in on himself like an armadillo.

Already? Sugar Plum glanced over her shoulder. Sure enough, the werewolf had finished its snack, and its still-ravenous attention had returned to the redheaded child.

Sugar Plum glanced at her bubblegum watch. "Not to worry," she said. "This is a dream. Time works strangely here. Observe."

The boy lifted his head, blue eyes peeking curiously out from his mop of copper curls as the werewolf inched forward, a low growl rumbling in its chest.

"Three ..." Sugar Plum kept count with her fingers, "two ... one."

The growl turned to a pained yelp, then a whimper, then a grotesque gag and a series of wet splashes. Sugar Plum's nose crinkled at the putrid scents that followed, and Eugene turned his suddenly green face aside, covering his mouth with a trembling hand.

"This brings me to our first lesson of the evening," Sugar Plum said. "Never, ever, ever feed a dog chocolate, unless that dog happens to be a vicious, twelve-foot-tall, anthropomorphic manifestation of your inner turmoil. Which brings me to my next point: werewolves typically ... Are you listening to me, Eugene?"

Sugar Plum snapped her fingers, and the boy's eyes tore away from the sickly monster that had again stolen his attention. He nodded, looking even more frightened of Sugar Plum than he'd been of the werewolf.

Sugar Plum relished the moment. Respect for her station was scant in the Kingdom Just Beyond a Star. She smoothed her skirt and cleared her throat. "Werewolves represent anger. Clearly, someone's rage has made a home inside your head—a strict teacher, a sibling, a school bully, etcetera. At any rate, you need to either confront them or tattle on them, and I highly recommend the latter given your ..." She waved a flippant hand at the still-shuddering boy, "*disposition*. If you keep quiet, you won't sleep through Christmas Eve, Santa won't leave presents, and *I* won't get my holiday bonus. I've been saving up for a vacation somewhere nice—Neverland, maybe, though I hear Narnia's pretty this time of year, now that they've taken care of their witch problem. You don't want to get in the way of my self-care, do you?"

Eugene blinked like a sputtering Christmas light, so Sugar Plum repeated herself. "*Do you?*"

The boy shook his head. His gaze returned to the monster that suffered behind Sugar Plum, squinting like he was trying to find the face beneath the fur. "W-will the chocolate kill him?"

"Oh, heavens no. Not so small a dose for so big a beast." Sugar Plum rifled through her bag again. "But this oughta do the trick!"

Eugene's eyes stretched to the size of saucers as she pulled her battle-axe from her bag—forged from a massive cherry-flavored lollipop and sharpened to a wicked gleam. The waking world must've been a bore, being subject to the laws of physics. A human could never store something twice their height in a container as small as their fist. *They must spend a fortune on luggage.*

"If the vomit made you queasy, you'll definitely want to close your eyes for this part," Sugar Plum warned.

She waited for Eugene to heed her advice, then hefted her axe over her shoulder, turning to face her foe. The werewolf was a pathetic echo of the beast it had been when she arrived—a heaving heap of tremorous fluff, whimpering pitifully from the center of a puke-puddle. That's all most rage was, when you boiled it down: fear in a fur coat, trying to look tough.

Sugar Plum leveled her axe with the creature's neck. She had to admit, she loved this part of her job, not for the power (though that was certainly a plus), but for the *knowing.* Someone had caused this kid a heck of a lot of worry. Whoever it was, she wanted to look them in their glassy, lifeless eyes before her time ran out.

"At least all dogs go to heaven," she lied and swung her axe forward.

Crystal candy cracked against the carpet, and scarlet spilled into the sick. Just like that, the wolf reverted, and Eugene's *real* nightmare made itself known.

Sugar Plum recognized those blue eyes, that red hair. An exact copy of each still cowered in the corner.

"Keep your eyes closed," she ordered Eugene, stepping between the boy and the body. With practiced indifference, she plucked the severed head up by the copper curls and plopped it into her side-bag, mourning the loss of a million hitherto-untouched toffies with a silent sigh. *I was due for a restock anyway.*

A familiar ballad began to weave through the room, slithering like the serpent it was. Sugar Plum was running out of time. She disposed of the body in the same manner she had the head (which took some maneuvering, magic or not), then fluttered casually across the room, hardly feeling heavier for the corpse in her satchel. The music followed after, stalking her.

"Ahem." She cleared her throat, alighting beside Eugene.

He looked up, tears glistening on his cheeks. He'd already known the werewolf's identity.

"Care to tell me why you're so angry with yourself?" Sugar Plum asked.

Eugene looked away, ashamed. "Dad's gone," he said. "Mom swears it has nothing to do with me, but ..." Eugene's shoulders dropped with the sentence.

Another of these ... Sugar Plum was no good at providing consolation. Despite her name, sweetness had never been her strong suit.

The music grew louder, the staccato scales of the celeste coiling tightly around Sugar Plum's waist, forcing her thoughts to her tongue. "Look ..." she said, still unsure where her sentence was headed. "You're only nine. This isn't your burden to—"

A terse tug, and Sugar Plum was hurtling through a starscape. Music whirled around her, dragging her through brights and darks and fields of cotton-candy clouds. By the time the song faded, she was home.

The savory aromas of fresh-baked pastries and simmering syrups wafted past Sugar Plum as she leaned against the bakery counter, waiting for Chef to work his magic in the kitchen beyond.

"You broke another?" asked Rose, examining a leafy hand as though she had nails to trim. "That's the eighth axe this month, Plum. Soon, Chef's gonna start charging for replacements."

"Charge *moi*?" Sugar Plum asked, eyelashes aflutter. "I'm too pretty to pay for things. Besides, I keep this place running. If the nightmares take over, there won't be any meadows left for you flowers to dance through. Mother Ginger would snap. Candy Cane Forest would be shattered to splinters. The Coffee Desert would go *decaf*." She feigned a swoon. "Who, then, would our precious Chef bake his treats for, hm?"

"The sole survivor, of course," Rose said, flipping a petal from her face. "Me."

Sugar Plum laughed rather than argue the point. She could easily have outlasted Rose in a survivalist situation, but they were equally matched for wit, and she wasn't in the mood for an inevitable stalemate. Besides, Rose was the only tolerable pick from the garden of dancing flowers, so Sugar Plum preferred to stay on her good side. Unlike Daisy, Bluebell, Peony, and Orchid, Rose had ... well, she had thorns. Sugar Plum preferred her friends sharp, even if that meant they were sometimes pricks.

"What'd you break your blade on this time, anyway?" Rose took sip of her Mandarin tea. "Zombie? Ghost? Vampire?"

"Another werewolf," Sugar Plum said with a sigh. "This upcoming generation is furious, and perhaps they have the right to be. Thing is, too many turn that anger inward." Sugar Plum thought back to Eugene, his own victim and tormentor. She hadn't had time to finish her lecture, and there would be no second session. One vision per little insomniac—that was the rule. She hoped she'd gotten her point across. If even a few words had stuck, she could believe her job was more than wanton violence.

"Oh, right," Rose said, shattering Sugar Plum's focus. "The whole 'dream therapy' thing. Don't suppose you've any evidence to support this theory of yours, do you, *Doctor Plum*?"

Sugar Plum hated when Rose called her that. Even if the Kingdom Just Beyond a Star offered a doctoral program, she could never have made time to attend classes. "I've read books." She snatched Rose's tea away and took a long drink.

"What kind of books?"

"The kind with spines and pages and covers." Sugar Plum set the empty teacup on the counter between them. "Anyway, it's practically common knowledge: monsters represent vices and societal ills, every last one of them."

"And werewolves are rage?"

"Werewolves are rage."

"What about Zombies?"

"Consumerism, obviously. Ever been to a Black Friday sale? Looks exactly like a zombie apocalypse, only the stakes are lower and there's less brains involved."

"Ghosts?"

"That one changes, person to person," said Sugar Plum. "Ghosts tend to represent guilt—crimes committed, promises broken, harsh words spoken in haste. Make no mistake, there's some stereotypical 'unfinished business' at the root of any haunting."

"What about vampires?" Rose asked.

"Not my department." Sugar Plum arched an eyebrow. "Vampires are strictly post-pubescent, and they aren't exactly nightmare material."

Her meaning hovered a bit before landing. When it finally did, Rose smirked like a dewdrop sprite. "On that note, how are things going with Cavalier?"

Sugar Plum bristled. Or she would have, were her perfectly coifed hair not slicked in place with treacle. She did not want to talk about Cavalier. He was much too ... *cavalier* about things. Relationships included.

Rather than respond, she turned and tapped the top of the tiny silver bell on the counter. A crystal note rang throughout the bakery, beckoning Chef from the kitchen. He emerged toting the most beautiful axe Sugar Plum had ever seen: candy-apple green, melting to raspberry red along the edges of the blades.

"I love it!" she squealed, clapping. "You've really outdone yourself, Chef!"

"If that's the case, I'll have to start charging you." Chef set the axe on the counter. "Myself is pretty competitive. If I keep outdoin' him, he'll resent me."

"I'm too pretty to pay for things."

Chef *harrumphed*, but he didn't disagree.

Sugar Plum lifted the axe from the countertop, marveling at its lightness and running a finger along a blade. It sliced her skin, finer than a papercut. "This'll do quite nicely."

New York had to be Sugar Plum's least-favorite place in the waking world. Sure, it looked pretty in the pictures, but so did great white sharks. Get close enough to either, and your reaction would be anything but *awww*.

It was the filth that bothered her most. She'd seen swamps with less slime and landfills with less litter. And that wasn't taking into account the metaphorical grime. Roaches skittered in the shadows as she fluttered through an apartment building which absolutely didn't meet fire codes, or safety codes, or *any* codes.

Typically, her clients were nearby when she arrived in a dream. This time, no sniveling child idled in the mildew-plagued hallway. Whoever Clara Stahlbaum was, she wasn't making things easy. Nor was her conspicuously quiet monster.

"I wonder what I'll face this time," Sugar Plum muttered, fingers already itching for her new axe. She hoped it would be something exciting. It had been a while since she'd last encountered a banshee; those were specific to Irish children dealing with anticipatory grief—a niche demographic. Kitsune were fun too, though they were vicious little bastards. Mischief was extra mischievous when you gave it a few fluffy tails and the power of illusion. Then, there were always good old-fashioned boogeymen: nothing to fear but fear itself, indeed.

Halfway through the mental catalogue of monsters, Sugar Plum heard faint sniffles wisp down the hall from beneath the door of the furthest apartment. As Sugar Plum fluttered closer, the sobs turned to a soliloquy.

"Leave him alone," a girl's voice whimpered. "Leave *us* alone ... please."

Ah—her cue. Sugar Plum patted her skirt, closed her eyes, then appeared on the other side of the door in a sudden spray of sparkles.

The room was teeming with rats. Hundreds of them—big as beagles and twice as tenacious. Rather than shrink back from Sugar Plum, they stretched forward, balanced precariously on their spindly, furless feet.

Perhaps they thought a meal had landed in their midst, or maybe they'd deemed her a nuisance ...

Either way, they'd started to salivate.

Just a nightmare, Sugar Plum reminded herself, careful to keep her toes from touching the grimy ground.

A door creaked, and she spun to see a girl of perhaps twelve peeking out from behind it. Clara. She was dressed in rags, save the baby-blue ribbons that adorned her frizzy black braids, and her lips trembled at the sight of the rats. Somewhere behind her, a toddler cried.

"You're here to help us?" she asked, eyes fixing on the fairy.

Sugar Plum nodded "This is a nightmare, and I'm a dream." She drew her candy-apple axe. "We tend to win out in the end."

Several rats sprang toward Sugar Plum, and she swung her weapon in a smooth arc, turning the nearest wall to a Pollock mural. Another slash, and a second wave was reduced to crimson mist. Unfortunately, more rats scurried forward, undaunted by the spray.

This was going to get annoying.

A screech split the night, originating somewhere behind Sugar Plum, and the scant hope in Clara's eyes fled all at once. "The Rat King," she whispered.

"It's ... it's just a nightmare," Sugar Plum assured her, though a few, un-moussed hairs at the nape of her neck stood straight with fright.

"It is." Clara took a step back. "And it isn't."

The door clicked shut.

A second screech, closer and more musty, bid Sugar Plum to turn and face her foe. When she did, a shiver of terror scurried down her spine. Where the other rats were beagles, this was a wolfhound. No, worse—it was the improbable spawn of a wolfhound and a hydra. And a rodent. And general unpleasantness. Its body was a massive, mangy mound of muscle, topped with ten heads and at least twenty twined tails. A rusty, scrap-metal crown glinted dully atop its centermost forehead, and quarter-machine rings adorned each of its boney fingers.

Sugar Plum flung her axe forward with panicked abandon, and a couple of rodential heads rolled on the floor, squeaking their last. Quick as they'd fallen, they began to regrow, sprouting from the creature's still bleeding neck. Only now, eight beady eyes glared out from where four had blinked before.

"Rats," cursed Sugar Plum, aware it was a little on the nose.

The creature lunged forward, pinning her to the floorboards by her wings. Her head smacked hard against the floor, and the room spun. Dreams weren't physically dangerous for the dreamer; for *visitors*, however ...

When her vision cleared, fourteen furry faces shrieked at her, washing her in blue-cheese breath, drool dripping from their jagged yellow teeth. Sugar Plum could easily have hacked a few of those faces away—miraculously, her axe remained securely in her grasp—but she'd learned from her previous mistake. Since fighting would land her in double the trouble and freezing was seldom helpful, she decided to go with option three.

"Time to flee," she said, disappearing in a silvery cloud.

She appeared in the bedroom beside Clara, startling the girl so that she bumped into a younger child, knocking him to the floor. Naturally, he began to cry, reminding the Rat King and his mousy minions of their presence. The fevered chorus that followed would have sent a horde of warriors crying for their mothers.

Somehow, a sonorous melody broke through the din.

"Not yet," Sugar Plum begged, pressing her back to the door right as something heavy slammed against it, straining the hinges and nearly knocking her to the floor. "I've never seen anything like that before!" She turned desperate eyes to Clara, who was still trying to comfort the crying boy—her brother, from the look of things. "Do *you* have any clue what it represents? Poor hygiene, perhaps? Rats steal things, right? Have you been stealing?"

"I'm not a thief!" Clara said, indignant. She briefly abandoned her brother to pull an ornate wooden doll from the overstuffed chest by the wall. The nutcracker, delicately carved and pristinely painted, looked like it might have been worth more than the building itself. She handed the toy to the boy, and his sniffles softened.

Sugar Plum tried to ignore the music, the screeching, and the scratching, her eyes narrowing on the nutcracker. "If you're not stealing, where did you get that?" she asked. "I know it's real. If you were going to gussy up the place, you'd have started by ridding it of rats."

"I didn't gussy anything, and I didn't steal neither!" Clara stomped her foot. "Our godfather's a toymaker, and he sends us presents sometimes. Besides, what's that got to do with the Rat King?"

The music grew louder, looping Sugar Plum's limbs and tightening. "This must reflect something! It's only a nightmare!"

"It is." Clara glanced around the musty, unlit room. "And it isn't."

The song reached its crescendo, and Sugar Plum was ripped away.

The chipper ditty of the dancing flowers followed Sugar Plum across the meadow, its notes clashing sorely with those of the merlot she'd had for breakfast. By contrast, Rose's questions weren't as annoying as they might have been. Still annoying, though.

"What in Santa's name has gotten into you?" she asked for the hundredth time as they breached the border of Candy Cane Forest. "You haven't told me where we're headed or why!"

Sugar Plum's trot slowed to a march, her stilettos sinking into a carpet of freshly fallen snow, and she released Rose's wrist. Already, the cloying scent of peppermint had sobered her. Pity. "We're going to visit Mother Ginger."

Rose stopped mid-stride, bursting into a melodic fit of giggles.

Unamused, Sugar Plum stomped away from her friend. She could not risk idling. If she idled, she might flutter right back to the meadow and dismiss her plan as a bout of random insanity. She wasn't sure she could live with that level of cowardice.

"I'm sorry!" Rose caught up, wiping a bemused dewdrop from her eye. "It's only that it isn't payday."

"Unfortunate, isn't it?"

"And you hate Mother Ginger."

"It's more that she hates *me*." And that hatred had probably tripled since Sugar Plum called things off with the woman's son.

"So, if she's not signing your paycheck and this isn't a social call ..."

Sugar Plum tried to steel her jaw; this wasn't the sort of story she could summarize vaguely, but she made the mistake of sighing, and the words spilled right out of her. They didn't stop until she'd told Rose all about Clara and her brother and the Rat King and her failure. By the end of the tale, tears played at the corners of her eyes. Thank Santa they froze before becoming obvious.

The tale left Rose quiet, but all silences break. "Why worry about it?" she asked eventually. "Ironically, you can't touch tangible problems, and it sounds like Clara's dealing with *actual* rats in the waking world. Why not leave those sorts of things to the parents?"

"She doesn't have any parents." Sugar Plum was certain of it, given the state of the apartment. Perhaps that's why this particular case bugged her so much: usually, if she failed a child, she trusted that someone else would look out for them. That wasn't the case this time around. *Unless* ... "She mentioned a godfather. Perhaps he can help them."

The two rounded a bend, and the spicy scents of ginger and nutmeg slammed into them, mixing with the peppermint in a nauseating fashion. A massive confectionary cottage loomed at the end of the path, its burnt-orange eaves dripping icing and tiled with colorful nonpareils. Even Rose gulped at the sight of it, and she rarely gulped anything but tea.

"Do we have to involve Mother Ginger?" she asked. "Why not just tell the girl to reach out to her godfather?"

Sound advice, but a little late. "One Sugar Plum vision apiece, remember?" she said, starting down the butterscotch stepping-stones which led to the door. "I'm just praying the godfather hasn't used his."

"You know who he is?"

"No. But I know he's a toymaker." Sugar Plum thought back to an overstuffed toy chest, surrounded by squalor. From its contents, only one item stuck with her—an archaic, overtly ostentatious relic from an age when pecans were considered treats. "I think he makes collectibles." She knocked on the door.

"And that helps because ..."

Before Sugar Plum could answer, the cottage door swung open. She'd been bracing herself for Mother Ginger's acerbic glare, so she was nearly relieved to be greeted by a familiar, pearly smile. Nearly.

Cavalier looked fashionable as always with his crisp navy tailcoat, slicked-back auburn hair, and carefree poise—all direct contradictions to the chaotic noises coming from the house behind him, which rivaled a circus both in volume and variety. "Back already?" he asked, his smile somehow stretching. "You must have missed me dearly, Sugar."

"That's not my name."

Cavalier shrugged. "It's part of your name." Something stampeded down a nearby hall, shaking the walls, but he hardly seemed to notice. "And if it weren't, it would still suit you. You're sweet and sparkly and—"

"About to leave you toothless." Sugar Plum's fingers folded into fists, but she managed to keep them at her sides. "Honestly, we didn't even know you'd be here."

"Wait ... *we*?" He peered around the door, spotting Rose. "Oh, hello! Been a while."

"I think I'm supposed to be angry with you," Rose said, not convincingly. A hopeless romantic, she'd always shipped Sugar Plum and Cavalier.

"Angry with *me*?" Cavalier looked nearly offended. "Because Sugar ditched me?"

"I didn't ditch you; I dumped you. And only after catching you with one of the Coffee Desert dancers."

"Is *that* what this is all about?" he asked, chuckling. "Macchiato and I were only dancing, darling; it's kind of what dancers are known for. Don't get me wrong—she's stimulating and compellingly bitter—but only *you* can sate my sweet tooth."

"For Santa's sake," Sugar Plum groaned, fighting an eye roll so dramatic it might have launched them from their sockets. "Even if I believed you—"

"Why settle for theories when you could hear a testimony? I'm sure Cappuccino would vouch for me, or Mocha, or Latte. We're all quite close."

Rose's palm hit her forehead. "Soooo not helping your case."

That it wasn't, but then, Sugar Plum wasn't exactly an impartial jury. "We're here to see your mother."

"She's on vacation in Narnia, and—

"Ah, yes—I heard they have an opening for a witch."

"—I've been tasked with babysitting while she's away." Something heavy crashed to the floor in the next room. "So, if you're not ready to make amends, I'd best check and see how many survived ... whatever that was." He started to close the door but paused. "You're positive there's nothing I can do to help?"

Sugar Plum pursed her lips, exhaling slowly through her nose. "I suppose there's one thing ..."

Adagios

Mother Ginger's doll collection was expansive enough to put the creepiest bed-and-breakfast to shame. On a normal day, the figurines were arranged by realm, designer, decade, year, and season. Sugar Plum wished she'd arrived on a normal day.

"What happened in here?" she asked, blinking at the muddled mounds of porcelain and plastic. Rows of shelves still lined the pinstripe-papered walls, but every figurine that had once rested atop them had found its way into the chaotic jumble on the floor. Apparently, Mother Ginger's octuplets had been making the most of her time away.

Cavalier—ever living up to his name—yawned. "Oh, I think I left two or three of them alone in here for some time. Mother will fix it when she returns."

"Which is ...?"

"Christmas Eve or thereabouts."

Sugar Plum couldn't afford to wait that long. Or rather, Clara couldn't. "Well, I suppose I have my work cut out for me then."

"We certainly do." Cavalier shrugged off his tailcoat and tossed it carelessly behind him. "What were we looking for, exactly?"

Cavalier liked to use the word "we" where Sugar Plum was concerned, regardless of her opinion on the matter. It was fast becoming her least-favorite pronoun. "If I needed help, I'd call on Rose."

"And leave my poor siblings in *my* care?" Cavalier gestured at the devastated parlor. "Mother made the same mistake. Look how it's going."

Something shattered sown the hall, and rather than shout, Rose giggled along with the children. She was nurturing by nature—far more so than Sugar Plum.

Deciding to let Rose be, she folded her wings back and started sorting through the rubble. She didn't tell Cavalier to leave, so he didn't. "I'm looking for a nutcracker, clothed in blue and buttoned in brass," she said, in case he felt like being useful for once.

Apparently, he did. He knelt nearby, and they sorted silently through the rubble for roughly five minutes. Then, one of the toy piles began to shift.

Sugar Plum flitted back, reaching for her axe. "Your mother didn't buy anything from Geppetto, did she?" she asked, shuddering. Ever since a disastrous trip to the Island of Misfit Toys, she'd hated living puppets with a passion.

"Um ... I don't think so." Cavalier stepped toward the stirring; he was far from courageous, but he wasn't cowardly either. Almost thoughtlessly, he scooped up an armful of dolls, and a small, nearly blue face peeked out from the pile. "Marzipan? What are you doing in this mess?"

The toddler gasped deeply before answering. "Been ... here ... days."

Sugar Plum glared at Cavalier, who chuckled nervously. "I'm certain she's exaggerating," he said, his voice decidedly *un*certain. He plucked the child free by the collar. "Anyway, you'd best go play with the others. Rose is visiting."

"We're saved!" the child shouted, rushing from the room.

Cavalier tugged on his bowtie. "She can't really have been there that long," he tried. "I saw her a few hours ago ... Or perhaps that was Bonbon ... maybe Merengue ..."

Sugar Plum might have wasted an hour lecturing him, had her attention not been captured by a brass-buttoned figure, glinting out from the hollow Marzipan had left behind. She plucked the nutcracker eagerly from the pile and examined it. It was even more fancy up close, with topaz eyes, a slender, upturned nose, and an impeccably painted suit. The words "Drosselmeyer's Toy Co." were printed in gold on the soles of its glossy black boots.

"Let's see—Droble, Drogenham, Droll ..." Sugar Plum ran a finger across a page of log WW/US/NY/D/18, growing a little more impatient with every passing surname. "Drosselmeyer, finally!"

Five Drosselmeyers currently lived in New York: Drucilla, Donald, Ethel, Gloria, and Veronica. While names could be deceptive, Sugar Plum was willing to bet Donald was the godfather in question. Luckily, the checkbox by his name was unmarked.

"Someone's a sound sleeper." She grinned. *This might actually work.*

"You're sure this is alright?" Cavalier asked. He'd followed her to Mother Ginger's office and was hovering just beyond punching range. "Your job is to visit the dreams of children. Only children."

"Technically, there's no rule against this." Sugar Plum clapped the book shut and shoved it back onto the shelf. "Why ask? Are you going to tattle?"

"What? No! It's just ... Oh, never mind." Cavalier crossed his arms, slumping against the nearest shelf and looking askance.

Sugar Plum clasped the talisman she wore around her neck (shaped like a gingerbread man to remind her who she worked for) and closed her eyes, repeating Donald Drosselmeyer's name like a mantra.

A familiar ballad wisped through the air around her—a timer set to ticking. It enfolded Sugar Plum, rising swiftly, drawing her in like an eddy.

Just as the kingdom lost its grip, something else grabbed hold. Sugar Plum's last thought, before being whisked away, was that, while Cavalier was not a deadweight just yet, that was subject to change.

Variations

"What in Santa's name were you thinking?" Sugar Plum snapped, unfurling her wings. The motion pushed Cavalier a good five feet away. As intended.

He composed himself quickly, taking a moment to preen his hair and straighten his vest, not bothering to take in their new environment. "No one's done this before," he said. "Do you want to be alone if it goes wrong?"

"That doesn't concern you."

"Of course it does. I—"

"No. It doesn't. Nothing does; it's right there in your name."

Cavalier frowned, looking at his feet. "I care about ... stuff."

"Ah, yes, stuff. Of course." Sugar Plum turned in a slow circle, deciding to ignore him in favor of her new surroundings.

They were even more unpleasant.

The cracked-earth expanse she'd found herself in was not similar to the soothing sandy seas of the Coffee Desert, nor did it reflect the painted limestone and scraggly shrubbery of waking-world wastelands. Rather, it was ... well, it was the sort of desert someone would imagine if they'd never actually been to one—dry and dismal and impossibly beige. This dream desert was densely populated, though not by cacti, cowpoke, or cartoon coyotes.

But by ghosts.

Hundreds and hundreds of ghosts, dressed in military uniforms spanning several decades.

While the ghosts shared the same iridescent green hue, they were clearly separated by sandbag walls a length of arid earth. Gunfire streaked between the barricades, and explosions sounded in the distance, flashing with yellow-white light. Within seconds, the warfare ceased, and the ghosts turned their gleaming, incandescent eyes to their uninvited guests.

Sugar Plum grabbed Cavalier by his arm and dashed for cover behind a nearby boulder, narrowly avoiding a sudden spray of bullets that would easily have turned them to Swiss cheese. *Good timing*, she thought.

"It's just a dream, right?" Cavalier asked, wide-eyed. "We can't get hurt here?"

Sugar Plum's head still ached from her altercation with the Rat King. She didn't need to tell Cavalier that—her silence said it for her.

"Well, that's unfortunate," he said, taking the news surprisingly well. "How are we going to get out of this one, do you think?"

Getting out? There was no guarantee. Sugar Plum had never faced *armed* phantoms before. She could only hope they had the same weakness as other ghosts. Weaknesses, weaknesses ...

"Salt," she muttered, opening her satchel.

"Uh ... what?"

Within seconds, she'd secured a decent stockpile of salted caramels and beachside taffy. "Just one of these is enough to dispel a spirit," she said. "Stay here, I'll clear a path."

"I don't think so! This whole 'dream hopping' thing was supposed to be my job. I think I can handle a few ghosts."

The whole dream hopping thing *wasn't* Cavalier's job because he hadn't cared to take it; hence, Sugar Plum's promotion. It was dangerous work, so she wasn't about to let some untrained, irresponsible—

Cavalier grabbed two handfuls of candy and disappeared around the boulder, prompting a second spray of gunfire. Panicked, Sugar Plum scooped up the rest of the ammunition and followed. Three phantoms rushed her, only to dissolve beneath a volley of salted sweets from Cavalier. Sugar Plum lobbed a few taffies of her own at the next wave, reducing them to wisps of spectral smoke. Together, they cut through the horde with startling ease, leaving a trail of colorful carnage in their wake.

Not that it mattered.

Sugar Plum's least-favorite aspect of nightmares was that they couldn't be altered without the dreamer's involvement. Because of this, every phantom she and Cavalier slew blinked back into existence moments later, visibly befuddled but otherwise unharmed.

By luck or serendipity, Sugar Plum spotted a skyscraper on the distant horizon. She was willing to bet she'd find Drosselmeyer somewhere inside it. "That way!" she shouted, flying forward as fast as her wings could manage while Cavalier did his best to keep up.

Bullets screamed past—lucky misses, really—and firelight flashed in Sugar Plum's periphery.

Nearly there ...

Quite close, in fact, when the dreamscape drowned beneath a blinding wash of light, and she was lost to a rain of rubble.

"Sugar ...?"

The voice was an echo, distant as a dream.

"Sugar ...?"

The voice stirred Sugar Plum's consciousness, but a few seconds passed before she remembered that dreams weren't very distant at all.

"Sugar, wake up."

At least, one of them wasn't. That realization forced her eyes open.

"You're okay!" Cavalier said, pulling her against him and waking hundreds of tiny bruises. "Thank Santa you're alright, Sugar!"

"No'myname," she slurred, pushing Cavalier, too weakly. He got the message and released her of his own accord. "W-what happened?"

"A grenade tried to get a little chummy is all," he said, offering her a hand as he stood. "We've made it into the building you spotted."

Begrudgingly, she accepted Cavalier's hand. He winced when she grabbed it. Seemed he hadn't made it out unscathed either. His hair was matted into odd angles and his suit was tattered. Bruised skin peeked from the tears in the fabric, coated in a thin patina of dust. Sugar Plum didn't like the idea of being protected, and she *loathed* the thought of being carried to safety, so she decided not to inquire any further.

The scenery roiled when Cavalier pulled her to her feet.

What ...?

Before it even had the chance to settle, it registered as strange. Freshly waxed floors, clean white walls, and the soothing hum of an air conditioner. Even the windows—conjoined panes of spotless glass that ran the full length of the hallway—were curiously unshattered, despite the war which raged beyond them. "Bit odd, isn't it?" Sugar Plum asked absently.

"I wouldn't really know," Cavalier chuckled as he looked out the window. But his face was dark. "Are dreams always this awful?"

Sugar Plum felt the strange compulsion to place a comforting hand on his shoulder. She resisted. "Not if I do my job right."

After a moment of uncharacteristic silence, Cavalier asked. "Don't these things usually have a time limit?"

"Thank Santa that Drosselmeyer's a heavy sleeper!" Sugar Plum started down the hall, her sense of urgency returning. She'd have flown, had her wings ached less bitterly. Frightened to flap them, she settled for sprinting. Every room she passed looked the same—darkened and empty—until she rounded the corner to find a chamber brimming with fluorescence. A gift shop, according to the sign mounted above the sliding glass door, though the shelves boasted only one item, ad infinitum.

"What's with all the nutcrackers?" Cavalier asked breathlessly, having finally caught up with her.

"Let's find out, shall we?" The sliding glass doors parted as Sugar Plum strode forward, into the supposed gift shop, and Cavalier followed as she wove her way through the shelves, eventually coming upon a man—not a ghost, but flesh and blood and designer silk—who stood in the rearmost aisle, staring out a window.

"Donald Drosselmeyer?" Sugar Plum called before she'd even neared him.

He glanced over his shoulder. Tears glistened in his salt-and-pepper lashes, blurring topaz eyes, rimmed red. "Who are you?"

"That doesn't matter," Sugar Plum said.

"I'm Cavalier," her accomplice blurted. "And this is Sugar Plum. We're here to fix your dream."

Puzzlement rippled across Drosselmeyer's face, and something cold swept in behind it. "See yourselves out, then," he said, returning his attention to the window. "Nothing here needs fixing."

"You're joking, right?" Cavalier marched past Sugar Plum, straight up to the man, and waved toward the world beyond the glass. "This isn't normal. It shouldn't be ..."

Sugar Plum inched forward, curious as to what had caught Cavalier's eye. A ghost stood just outside the building, staring straight at Drosselmeyer. Unlike the others, he was far from menacing with his pressed fatigues, flushed face, and innocent smile.

"Who is—"

From nowhere, a bullet caught the soldier's chest, turning his uniform luculent scarlet. He fell on his back on the desert floor, and Sugar Plum flinched back. When she opened her eyes, the soldier was standing again, smiling again, his jacket clean and pressed. Until it wasn't.

Another fall. Another flinch. Another smile.

"How many times have you watched this happen?" Sugar Plum asked, entranced by the morbid cycle.

"Not enough," replied Drosselmeyer.

A strange answer. Too bad an unwelcome melody had drifted into the gift shop, leaving little time for questions.

"Look, I'd love to dissect your little vengeance show, or whatever you've got going on here, but we're pressed for time," Sugar Plum said. "Here's the gist: ghosts are guilt. Either you've done something you shouldn't have, or you didn't do something you should have, and you'll be haunted until you can make amends for it. As it happens, I know just how to go about that."

"I shouldn't have let him go," Drosselmeyer said, voice pinched. "I used to tell him stories about my time in the service; made it sound like the most glorious thing in the world. That's the thing about stories, especially true ones: we polish them up before presenting them—make them look shiny and clean, worthy of admiration." Outside, the soldier fell. Then rose. "You'd never know, as a listener, about all of the blood ..."

Not vengeance, after all. Sugar Plum glanced at the resurrected spirit, finding that he shared Drosselmeyer's topaz eyes and slender, upturned nose. Not *just* Drosselmeyer's. "You modeled the nutcracker after your son," she said.

"That's why you don't want our help," Cavalier interjected. "If you keep having this nightmare, you keep getting to see him again."

Drosselmeyer nodded, pensive. "As I said, you can see yourselves out."

They wouldn't need to see themselves anywhere at the rate that melody was swelling.

"Listen to me!" Sugar Plum grabbed Drosselmeyer by the chin, forcing him to meet her eyes. "I am sorry for your loss, truly, but your godchildren need your help."

"Clara and Fritz?" His forehead wrinkled. "They're fine. Their parents are—"

"Gone. I don't know how or why, but I know it's true."

Sadness flooded Drosselmeyer's eyes, only to freeze over. "I can't help them." He tore away. "I've already failed one child."

Sugar Plum was out of arguments, so she settled for seething. "Fine!" she snapped, shoving a salted caramel into Drosselmeyer's hand. "If you ever decide to end this haunting, you now have the means. In the interim, I hope you can sleep with your decision."

The candy dropped to the floor, but Sugar Plum kept marching toward the music. She was halfway down the aisle when she noticed Cavalier hadn't followed. *Let the nightmare have him, for all I care.*

She dismissed the thought immediately, whirling around. She might not have been sweet, but she wasn't *that* sour.

Cavalier still stood beside Drosselmeyer, speaking too softly to hear, especially over the still-growing ballad. Fresh teardrops streamed down Drosselmeyer's cheeks, flashing red from the distant firelight. Whatever Cavalier was trying at was working.

But they didn't have time for it.

The music swirled around Sugar Plum, latching to her ankles. She fought against it, desperately beating her injured wings. Pain swelled in her shoulder blades and spilled down her spine, but she fluttered forward anyway. Somehow, she managed to grab Cavalier's arm right as the song's tendrils tightened, dragging them home.

Coda

Sugar Plum stayed in bed a little late ... perhaps a few hours, perhaps a few days. With the shades drawn, it was hard to tell. Somewhere, children were probably losing sleep over her absence, but what did that matter? Their parents would comfort them. Or they wouldn't.

When someone knocked on her door, she tried to ignore it. When the knocking grew louder, she practically smothered herself with her pillow. When a second set of knocks joined the first, she resolved that a threat or two—possibly enacted—would better ward off visitors.

Rose and Cavalier waited on Sugar Plum's stoop— Rose with a platter of Chef's butterscotch cookies, Cavalier with an uninvited (though secretly appreciated) hug.

"What are you doing here?" Sugar Plum asked, deciding not to threaten her well-meaning friends after all. "It must nearly be Christmas Eve by now. Haven't you got a tree lighting ceremony to go to? A candlelight service? A—"

"We're not going to any of those without you!" Rose interrupted, shoving the cookies forward. Sugar Plum accepted them, smiling feebly, and set them on the shelf beside the door, where they were doomed to stale.

"I'm not in any mood to go out," she said. "I appreciate the check-in, though."

She reached for the doorknob, but Cavalier caught her hand. "We're worried about you," he said.

Sugar Plum found it strangely difficult to pull away. Apparently discerning as much, Rose smirked. "I just remembered! I have to go ... um ..."

"To meet my siblings at the tree lighting?" Cavalier offered, too readily.

"Yes, that!" The words had barely left her lips, and she was already at the end of the walkway. "Toodles!" she called back before disappearing into a world of freshly fallen white.

"Wait!" Sugar Plum called. "I—"

"Give me a few minutes." Cavalier squeezed her hand. "Please."

Sugar Plum was too tired to think up any good excuses. "I'll put some tea on."

"I prefer coffee."

"Macchiato, perhaps?"

Cavalier ignored the dig, sidling past her and throwing open the nearest curtains. "Please tell me you haven't been sulking in darkness this whole time."

"I haven't been sulking in darkness this whole time," Sugar Plum parroted.

"Funny." Cavalier settled into the sofa, patting the cushion to his right.

"No coffee, then?"

He shook his head, offering a ghost of a smile. Sugar Plum supposed it wouldn't kill her to sit beside him, given all she'd recently survived.

"You never asked what happened with Drosselmeyer," he said, once she'd joined him on the couch.

"That's because I know what happened: he chose his nightmares over his godchildren." Sugar Plum steeled herself, unwilling to cry no matter how her eyes burned. "Clara and Fritz are on their own. I accomplished nothing. *We* accomplished nothing."

Silence, thick as molasses, spread between them. Until Cavalier draped an arm over her shoulders. "Maybe not all monsters need slaying. Have you ever thought of that?"

"What?" Sugar Plum met his eyes, tempted to shrug him away. "Why?"

"Because I brought that possibility up with Drosselmeyer, and he seemed to agree." Cavalier pushed his hair out of his eyes with his free hand. Sugar Plum hadn't noticed, until then, that it wasn't slicked back. His suit was on the casual side, too—no vest or cuff links or ridiculous ribbon bowtie. "I couldn't fault him for wanting to remember his son. If I lost ... someone I cared about—*really* lost them, not just to a petty fight—I'd want to remember them too, only not by grief alone. I'd want to remember the smiles and laughter and warmth, the things we forget to be grateful for until they've long passed."

"You'd choose to be happy in mourning?" Sugar Plum arched an eyebrow. "Isn't that a little—"

"Cavalier?"

"I was going to say *impossible*."

Cavalier shook his head. "I think ghosts, of all monsters, are the most malleable—that we have a say in their shape and their color. Drosselmeyer's son would have wanted to be remembered, not for dying, but for living. I told the man as much, and he said he'd try to change the shape of his ghost."

"You ... think it worked?" Sugar Plum asked, more hopeful than she'd have admitted aloud.

Cavalier grinned. "Why not ask Clara?"

Sugar Plum deflated. How many times did she have to explain the rules? "Clara's used up her Sugar Plum vision," she said. "And now Drosselmeyer has too."

"Now, who said anything about a *Sugar Plum* vision?" Cavalier reached beneath his collar, pulling out a gingerbread talisman.

Sugar Plum's eyes widened. "You didn't ..."

"Mother's been begging me to join the family business for years." He shrugged. "I finally acquiesced ... on one condition."

"And what might that be?"

"That little Clara Stahlbaum get a second session." He grinned broadly. "Actually, it's Clara Drosselmeyer now, according to the logs."

"Does ... does that mean what I think it means?"

"That he adopted the kids? Well, I'm not really up on waking-world law, but that sounds about right to me."

Something strange possessed Sugar Plum in that moment. Before she could think better of it, she threw her arms around Cavalier, planting a kiss on his cheek.

"I see you're happy with the outcome." He blushed brightly. "Would you like to pay her a visit anyway?"

Sugar Plum nodded, closing her eyes, and the music swept them away.

... Curtain ...

Lilla Glass
Bio

Lilla Glass is an author from Olympia, WA. While fantasy is her first love, she dabbles in horror, sci-fi, and the occasional (gasp) non-speculative work. In winter 2021, she signed a four-book deal with City Owl Press for her darkly whimsical high fantasy series, *The Reel of Rhysia*. The first installment, *The Unseen*, is set to be released in July 2023.

Her short story *Best Spuds* was a Silver Honorable Mention in the Writers of the Future Winter 2021 Quarter competition. Find out how to get a copy at her website. Lilla has three other short stories in anthologies in 2021: *Thaw* for Mystic Owl Press, *The Faerie Ring* for Madhouse Books, and *Fresh Game* in *13 by 11* for Papillon du Père Publishing.

In the rare event that she isn't writing, Lilla works one of those pesky day-job thingies, reads stories and poetry that she wishes she wrote, hangs out with her husband, bunny, and cat, and tosses herself into the occasional mosh pit.

Visit Lilla's website for news about her activities

LillaGlass.com

Follow Lilla on Twitter

@lilla_glass

A TINTORETTO OF THE SOUL

EROL ENGIN

I was down on my luck. I'd called Jen up that morning and asked—nay, *begged*—if I could hang out at her place for a few days until I got my act together. I didn't tell her everything, but this time I really was stuffed.

My roommates'd had a gutful, and after a big roundtable discussion it was decided that I was *persona non grata*. It was about the usual things—not paying my share and running up bills—but it was also about *trust*, they said, the sanctimonious bastards. They couldn't trust me anymore.

I packed up and, not thinking about where I was going to sleep that night, left. I tried a few avenues before Jen without success, but as luck would have it, she and her husband Ralph were going to Melbourne for a weeklong conference, so they (or more precisely Ralph) wouldn't have to suffer my physical presence. I was truly grateful.

It was a pretty cool pad, I had to admit: a warm condo-style apartment in Bondi, not quite overlooking the beach, but nearly. It had sun-lights and a bank of panoramic glass doors that kept the place lit and cozy all day, even in the depths of nippy winter. The glass doors opened onto what was, for my money, the best feature of the condo: a low-walled patio that Jen had stocked with grevilleas and other native plants. I couldn't help but picture the Sydney literati there, Jen moving amongst them with charm and ease, playing the affable host at a party or book launch. Back at uni, I'd been the one with the great future, but it was Jen who'd ended up doing well for herself as an agent.

I wandered over to the patio, opened the glass doors, and stepped out into the sun. Though I was surrounded by other similar apartment blocks with patios, I seemed to be the only one 'taking the air.' It was a beautiful day. Generally, I'm not given to self-reflection (it too often doubles as self-pity), but as I gazed out at trendy Bondi, I couldn't help but feel the keen sting of my own Loserdom. How had I got to this point? How had I become a fraction shy of a pitiable couch-surfer? Me, Gus Anderson, of whom there had once been great expectations?

It all came down to one thing: luck.

Jen had said it herself. A year ago, she'd taken me out for dinner to a swanky place in Leichhardt and let me down easy just before dessert. She couldn't pedal my novel anymore, she said, the novel she'd taken on as yet another favor to me, her loser ex-boyfriend from uni. It was an 'unlucky time,' the publishers that she'd pitched to had 'just put out very similar books' (but probably better, I thought, reading between the lines), the 'market was glutted,' 'in turmoil,' and not really receptive to 'such a cerebral exploration of modern relationships.' Could I write something more 'book club'? Maybe a 'Christmas romance'? Christ!

I've replayed that dinner in my head a thousand times. What if my luck had been different? What if Jen had told me that my novel had been accepted? I could have been a success. Not a million-seller, granted, but maybe a prestige author. If only I'd had luck.

If only.

I was interrupted from these musings by a frantic hammering at the door. I considered pretending I wasn't at home, but the knock was too insistent to ignore. I stubbed out my smoke and wandered back inside.

'Alright, hold on!' I called out. 'Jesus!'

I opened the door and stood staring at a chunky little woman with a wide, attractive face and big green eyes. She wore a lawn-green headscarf that appeared too tight: the hem had left a series of angry red creases streaking like welts across her forehead.

'You're here!' the woman said, rapturously. 'You're finally here!'

She clasped her hands together and held them close to her ample bosom. An assortment of bangles slid down her forearms and collected in the crooks of her arms.

'I'm so glad to see you! You simply *can't* know how long I've been waiting.'

'I can't?'

'No,' she said. 'You can't!'

She began a mad search for something in her shoulder bag.

'Oh, where *is* it?' Don't tell me you've been a dodo, Daphne, and left it downstairs. Daphne the dodo, that's what Frank used to say. *Got it! Got it!*'

She retrieved a slender book and held it out for me to take. Her round face and wide eyes beamed up at me with the force of a cracked spotlight.

I accepted the book. What choice did I have? As soon as I took it in my hands, Daphne began backing away down the hall.

'Oh, I can't do it,' she said. 'I thought I could, but I can't!'

She continued to recede, staring at me as though I might at any moment vanish. Before she reached the elevator, she very quickly waved at me and then disappeared into it, leaving me standing at the door, holding the book, wordless.

I went back inside and battled with Jen's espresso pumper until it yielded a sludgy ristretto. Not loving the coffee beans' seasonal spice too much, I stood in the kitchen sipping it, wondering if my day could get any stranger. As the caffeine began to hit, I took my first real look at the book this strange woman had given me.

It was a volume of poetry, called *Inferno*, and the author was a guy called Andy Gustafson. I'd heard of him, but vaguely. I flipped to the author bio and my eyes rested on the photo there. The thin, almost greasy-looking dark hair, the swollen cheekbones, and deep-set eyes—not to mention the pasty, pockmarked skin—were, at a glance, remarkably similar to my own. I am not a pretty face, and neither was this Andy fellow, no matter how flattering the light or creative the photographer. Clearly, Daphne had mistaken me for him. As I examined the book, two photo-sized pieces of paper slid out onto the kitchen bench.

They were photos of Daphne. Naughty photos. Selfies, actually. In one, she was in garish Christmas-red lingerie, her tongue poking out through painted lips, *Inferno* practically wedged down her cleavage. The other one was ... well, especially daring. She reclined in bed, fixing the viewer with an insatiable stare, a hill of snow-white and red satin pillows glistening luridly behind her. In one hand she held *Inferno*, but the other lingered above her lace panties, her fingertips nudging suggestively under the frill. She had written 'Happy Christmas! For Your Eyes Only' on the backs of the selfies, along with her contact details. She lived in the apartment below Jen's.

I nearly jumped when my mobile went off.

'Gus, how are you?'

It was Jen. She'd hardly been gone three hours and already she was calling to check up. I had to give myself a shake before I was ready to talk.

'You can tell Ralph I haven't gone berko,' I said.

She told me all about what was happening in Melbourne. They'd barely touched down, but she and Ralph were already having a fabulous time. She did have a bit of a sniffle though, but it would probably go away. She rabbited on, and I listened patiently, waiting for the opportunity to ask her the question I really wanted to ask. Finally my window of opportunity arrived.

'Jen,' I said, trying to sound disinterested, 'who is that kooky soul that lives downstairs?'

'Oh, that'd be Daphne.' Jen sighed. 'Her husband left her six months ago. It's hit her pretty hard.'

'Bit of a cracked egg.'

'Wrong season. She's lovely, Gus, really, really lovely. And she loves poetry. Be kind to her, Gus, she deserves it.'

'Oh, I will,' I said, 'I will. I might invite her up for dinner later on, if that's OK with you.'

'Sure.'

'By the way, Jen, are you expecting any other guests? Some poet guy? Daphne mentioned him.'

She paused for a moment and then remembered. 'Andy Gustafson!' she said. 'I almost forgot. But he shouldn't be staying until next week. He's coming for the Writers' Festival.'

'Daphne seems to have mistaken me for him,' I said. 'Isn't that a hoot?' I explained about the book, but no way did I tell her about my early Christmas gift, the photos inside.

We chatted for a while longer. When we were finished, I put my mobile down on the countertop. I stared at it for maybe five seconds.

Then I grabbed it and tapped in Daphne's number.

I don't get much, if you know what I mean. As I said before, I'm not a looker, and I'm not successful. My only chances are with women I meet at parties who don't know me or any of my friends or acquaintances and who are blissfully ignorant of my Loserdom. Usually, I'll pretend to be a writer, and with any luck, they won't twig to my act until it's too late. Right or wrong, that's how I roll.

So it wasn't really that much of a stretch to invite Daphne up and pretend to be Andy Gustafson. Usually, I just pretend to be a writer; with Daphne, I was pretending to be a *specific* writer. A little more challenging, granted, and a lot more dishonest. But, as I saw it, this value-added deceit was still well within my bullshit range.

I approached my new role like a real actor. I spent time researching my character, scouring the Net for tidbits that might make my performance more convincing. By dinnertime, I had Andy down—including his somewhat effeminate hand gestures and slight lisp—so that only his mother could tell us apart.

When she came up, I noticed that Daphne had added a cape to her general Blavatsky outfit, and I think she'd done something unfortunate to her hair. It was a brilliant orange, very short and styled into peaks like sharp little eruptions from a solar surface. I tried not to stare.

Dinner was a breeze. Being Andy, I found it easy to turn on charm that I didn't know I had. And Daphne was pretty good company, too. Her readiness to laugh made up for a tendency toward bizarre non-sequiturs. Whenever the conversation lagged, she would mutter odd words and phrases, such as 'cummerbund,' as if she were trying to cast a spell. Despite this, we talked mostly about poetry and poets (Daphne favoring Maya Angelou). The naughty photos lurked unspoken, and thus highly conspicuous, behind every word.

It was when dinner came to an end and we were sitting close together on the couch sipping Irish coffees (the Christmas spice almost, but not quite, ruining them) that we suddenly stopped talking. Our eyes met, and the next thing I knew, Daphne and I were pawing at one another like teenagers on a babysitting date. We retired to the bedroom, dropping clothes as we went. While I'm not complaining, the sex was of the sweaty and grunty variety, full of bed-shaking histrionics and very ... let's say 'non-Christmas-movie' dialogue (Daphne at one point throwing her head back and exclaiming, 'Bone me, Andy!').

After the third time, I was relieved to start some pillow talk.

'I hope you didn't think I was too ... forward?' she said, referring to the photos.

'Nope.'

'Well, that's the new me,' she said, 'the new Daphne. She goes for it. She knows what men want and she goes for it.'

Then it all came pouring out. She told me the story of how her husband had left her. The upshot of it was that they had grown apart and he'd found someone else.

'I'm sorry to hear all that,' I said.

'Andy, I ...'

She cut herself off. Her face clouded over and seemed to split in half, one side battling Gollum-like with the other. At one point, she shook her head and whispered, 'No, that's what the old Daphne would do!' It was like watching a ventriloquist act that had no dummy. 'Andy,' she said, finally, 'you could help me.'

'Help you, Precious?' I said, a bit warily. Helping people was not my forte.

'With your poetry. You could win Frank back for me with a poem, maybe even in time for Christmas. You're so fortunate to have that talent, Andy. A poet is like ... being a Tintoretto of the soul. Wouldn't you agree?'

'Sure, but ...'

'Do you think you could do that? Write a poem so powerful it would bring him back?'

'Well, Daphne ...'

'You know,' she said, sitting up, 'something like you did with *Inferno*, something deep and swirling, a witch's incantation of a poem. Deep. Profound. Mysterious. Like "Love Itself," Andy.'

I thought to myself, *Jesus*.

There was no stopping her now. The words came tumbling out.

'I could give the poem to Frank, you see, and pretend it was from me. The poem would be full of secret things, powerful things—phrases, images, memories—that only Frank and I would know. I could write those things out and you could toss them into the bubbling cauldron of your imagination. If you could do this, Andy, I'd be so grateful. There's no underestimating the power of poetry. And isn't it the season of miracles? I know my plan isn't strictly ...' She stopped to shrug her shoulders. 'Strictly ...'

She couldn't seem to find the word.

'Legit?' I offered.

'Legit! Yes, that's it! It's not strictly legit. But all's fair in love and war,' she said, her voice a seductive purr.

'And poetry,' I added.

We did it again. Daphne called out this time for Frank to bone her and tears began to stream down her face. I don't think they were orgasmic tears. I wondered if I would ever hear a lover yell 'bone me, Gus.'

I decided that it didn't really matter and concentrated on the task at hand.

The next morning I woke up feeling hungover and leather-mouthed. I hadn't had a night of such sexual abandon since ... well, let's just say too long. Daphne had worn me out. I went to the kitchen and went *mano a mano* with the coffee machine again. This time it yielded a tepid non-potable sludge, so I settled for instant. On my way to the couch, I spied something lying on the floor. An envelope, slipped under the door.

Daphne?

I walked over and picked it up. Inside was a letter, written in curly estrogen-fueled handwriting. It seemed to be a list of disjointed phrases and descriptions, but I had no idea what they meant. Then it hit me: it was Daphne's list of 'secret stuff, powerful stuff.'

I think I audibly groaned. When I agreed to her request, I'd thought it was just one more nutty inspiration that ran through her mind at any given moment. But, judging from the comprehensive list, it appeared that Daphne was serious. I gazed at it, wondering how in hell I was supposed to make poetry out of words like *cummerbund, gefilte fish, reindeer,* and, amazingly, *ichthyosaur.* No, I would have to go back and tell her the deal was off. I'd make up something, like I was in the middle of a set of cantos and my focus and creativity simply could not be diverted. Or that I'd simply just reconsidered. She would just have to lump it.

Breaking it off is probably what a sensible person would have done. But like I mentioned before, I don't get much. Breaking it off would mean no more Christmas boning. Daphne was not really a preferred partner, but I wasn't in a position to choose. Wouldn't it be easier, I wondered, just to knock a poem up, so I could continue doing the same to Daphne? It would be even easier, now that I was thinking about it, to cheat. I could turn to the Bard, to Keats, to Wordsworth, and for a bit of eastern exoticism, Rumi would be my man. We'd have another bonk session, perhaps two, then I would palm the poem off to her and by the time anyone was the wiser I would be on my not-so-merry way. Ho-ho.

This, I decided, was the way forward. A win-win solution: Daphne would get her poem, and I would continue, at least for the next day or so, to get laid.

I set about my task with gusto. I got on the Net and began to lift the best lines from my trusted sources. I chose lesser-known works, of course, to crib from, and vanity dictated that I steal from a few of my own poems (yes, I once considered myself a poet, too). By midday I'd finished a first draft and was very pleased with my morning's fraudulent effort.

Just as I was sitting back and enjoying a well-earned ciggie, the intercom buzzed. I sauntered over to it and pressed the talk button. I expected it to be Daphne, but the voice that came over the system was halting and a bit shy.

'Oh ... uh ... hi, I'm Andy. Andy Gustafson?'

I couldn't believe my lousy luck.

There I was, performing to the height of my abilities as a counterfeit poet, and the real author just had to come along and ruin it.

'Did Jen tell you I was coming?'

'Yeah,' I said, speaking into the intercom. 'But not till next week.'

'Oh. Well. I ...'

I buzzed him in—seasonal goodwill unto others, and all that. Or more that I had no choice: I didn't want him standing down there at the entrance where Daphne might see him. While he was coming up, I checked my phone. Sure enough, there was a message from Jen. There'd been a change of plans and Andy had to arrive in Sydney early. Her tone of voice sounded relieved that I would no longer be the sole custodian of her home. I paced about the living room, wondering how on earth I was going to tell him about Daphne. A moment or so later, Andy knocked on the door.

I opened it and stood face to face with the man I had been impersonating. I'd done him justice. Too much, in fact. My Andy had presence, charm, and even a lady-killing charisma. The man who stood in front of me was a weedy little pony-tailed twerp, puffed up in a battered North Face jacket, hiking boots, and cargo pants. With his Trotskyish glasses and goatee, there was a whiff of the lefty socialist about him, but mostly he emitted a dull carbon-tax activist, David Suzuki vibe. When I offered coffee, he asked if I had any roasted dandelion.

'Some what?' I said.

'Roasted dandelion,' he said, peeling off his jacket. 'It's a coffee substitute.'

'Bet it's shite,' I said, and, after he declined the sadly seasonally spiced & spruced beans, I made him a decaf instead.

For me, I made a double-strength ristretto. I figured that I would need the fuel. I came back to the patio and gave him his mug of neutered Joe. He raised his fine little hands and took the mug from me very graciously, nodding his head in appreciation. He sipped it and smiled and looked as content as if I had fed him a three-course meal.

'Just the way I like it, Gus,' he said. 'You're a master.'

I shrugged my shoulders. 'It's only decaf.'

His Weary Traveler act irked me; he'd only come from Brisbane, for Chrisakes, not the Himalayas. His presence had really put me out. I glared at him as he shared a story, in a quiet lisping voice, about a party Jen had thrown here on the patio where she'd spilt red wine all over Peter Carey's trousers. I told him a few mild tales from our uni days. When the conversation slowed, I said that I'd read *Inferno*.

'Oh,' he said, in mock horror, covering his mouth with his hands. '*That*. What can I say? It was my first collection. Pretty try-hard stuff.'

'I'll say. More of a sausage-sizzle than an inferno.'

If he was offended, he didn't show it.

'It was the best I could do at the time,' he said through a smile.

'You know, Andy, I'm a poet as well.'

'Are you?' he said, brightly, sitting up like a schoolboy getting Christmas pudding for dessert.

I hadn't really written any poetry for years, but I told him about my work. To my surprise, he seemed genuinely interested.

'You'll have to let me read some, Gus,' he said. 'Sounds like great stuff. Have you tried to publish any of it?'

I shifted in my seat and told him my tale of woe. I described one more time that soul-crushing dinner with Jen.

Andy shook his head. 'Bad luck, mate.'

I was tired of playing nice.

'Funny you should mention luck, Andy,' I said, 'I have this theory.'

He raised his eyebrows.

'The only difference between a published and unpublished author is luck.'

'Luck *is* important,' he admitted, wagging his head.

'No, Andy, it's not just important. It's the only difference.'

'What about talent?'

'Talent is subjective, and again, it's luck.'

He pursed his lips. 'I don't know ... talent is luck, but only to an extent. But what someone lacks in talent, or luck, one can make up for in hard work. That's what I believe.'

Suddenly I was inspired. 'Care to put my theory to the test?'

'What do you mean?' He seemed a little irritated now, which pleased me.

I told him about Daphne. I didn't feel squirmy or sheepish; in fact, you might say that I reveled in what I saw as my own slyness. I don't think Andy shared that interpretation.

'Jesus,' he said when I'd finished. 'You're kidding, right?'

'Unfortunately, no.'

'You pretended to be me so you could sleep with a woman?'

'Correct.'

He shook his head in disbelief. 'That's appalling.'

I took a long drag on my ciggie and let the smoke out through my nose in thin gray streams. I wanted him to think, *This bloke's a badass.* He probably wasn't aware of it, but there was just the tiniest hint of uncertainty, even fear, in his eyes.

'You're telling me you wouldn't have slept with her? That you'd knock back a sure thing like that—and at *Christmas*?!'

'That isn't the point.'

'Got a girlfriend?'

'No, but ...'

'I rest my case. Now, this is what I really wanted to tell you.'

I told him about the poem Daphne wanted me, or really *him*, to write.

Andy was horrified. 'That's an offense against poetry. A terrible abuse.' He seemed at a loss for words. 'I can't even begin to say how ... Even if the husband came back to her it would be based on a deception. It couldn't last. I would never have agreed to use poetry like that, Gus.'

I realized then that Daphne had been manipulating me as much—maybe even more—than I had her.

'You're like me, mate. You're no Lord Byron. You don't get much. So you take it whenever it comes.'

This was too much, even for Andy.

'Look, Gus, I've got a lot of work to do,' he said, plunking his decaf down and rising from the table. 'I'm giving a talk on landscape poetry tomorrow at GleeBooks. I'd better get something prepared. Thanks for the coffee.'

'Do you want to see the poem you wrote for her this morning?'

He lingered over the table, and I handed him the poem.

'It's weird,' he said once he'd read it. 'What's all this stuff about ichthyosaurs?'

I explained about Daphne's list.

'It's not bad, I guess,' he said.

'You could do better?'

'I really don't know, Gus.' He handed the poem back. 'Like I said, I've got work to do.'

I was in danger of losing him.

'I've had a bolt, Andy. We could each write a poem to give to Daphne. I'll say that I came up with two but couldn't decide which was better. The choice could be hers. What do you say?'

'What do I say? I say, why on earth would you want to do that?'

'To test my theory, of course. If Daphne chooses mine, it proves what I'm saying about luck and being published. If she chooses yours, it shows I'm full of shite.'

My being full of it was never really in question, Andy's expression told me. But he didn't say it; he just shook his head.

'Sorry, Gus. I can't be a party to this. Poetry—creativity—is a sacred thing. It shouldn't be used for impure or dishonest purposes. I'm sorry but I can't help you. And I've got plenty of work to do.'

He went off to unpack his things, leaving me standing on the patio.

I lingered there, reviewing the situation. I was quite impressed with my performance. Though it hadn't snagged an agreement from Andy, it had revealed at least one useful thing: like all writers,

Andy was vain. What really irked him was not that I'd impersonated him to sleep with Daphne, but that I, acting as Andy Gustafson the poet, was going to write her a poem. *That* was what really got to him. My evidence? When I showed him the poem I'd cribbed, the look he gave me said, *You can pretend to be me, Dick's quill, but you can't pretend to be the real poet.*

Pure writerly vanity.

This was the angle to exploit. Now I just needed a pretext with which to engage the enemy. I decided to bring him a bit of lunch. I worked diligently preparing sandwiches and more coffee (well, more of that dandelion dreck), humming away to myself. I was relishing what the near future held in store. When I was ready, I had a bracing smoke, stubbed out my ciggie, and knocked on Andy's door.

'Room service!'

The door opened. Andy looked at the tray I was carrying.

'Wow,' he said. 'Thanks.'

He tried to take the tray from me, but I squeezed past him and placed it on the bedside table. In the corner was an old-fashioned rolltop desk. Andy's laptop was fired up on it.

'Doing some writing?' I asked.

'Like I said, Gus, I have a lot of work to do.' He stood by the door, waiting to usher me out, but I wasn't ready to go. Next to his laptop was a picture in a frame, a photo of Andy as a teenager.

'You have a picture of yourself on your desk?'

'Yeah,' he said. 'For inspiration.'

'Just yourself. Nobody else?'

Again, he nodded.

'Dude,' I said, 'that's messed up.'

He drew a deep breath. 'I wouldn't expect you to understand.'

'You're right there, I don't.'

'If you must know, I keep it as a reminder of a promise I made to myself.'

He walked over to the desk, sat down, and picked up the photo. He seemed to consider for a moment, and then, in an against-my-better-judgment tone of voice, he launched into a story that might have been called 'Portrait of the Artist as a Sulky Teenager.' On a miserable school trip to the Blue Mountains one winter, he promised himself to become a writer.

'Before me was the green sweep of forest around the Sisters. I couldn't see them; they were shrouded in early morning mist. And I said to myself, "I'm going to be a writer." I actually said it out loud. When I did, the mist suddenly cleared, and the Sisters were revealed in all their natural beauty. Gus, I was stunned. I couldn't explain how I felt. Some kind of mysterious power thrummed through me, as if I'd become a conduit, or a vessel of some kind ...'

Yada, yada, yada. When he'd finished, I said, 'Very impressive, young Skywalker,' and made a wheezing noise like Darth Vader.

A beat or two of stunned silence followed.

Struggling to keep his voice even, he said, 'I was going to suggest that we work on the poem together, Gus, but clearly that's not possible. I think you should leave now.'

He raised an arm and pointed to the door. I stayed where I was. He swiveled huffily round in his chair.

'I checked your poem out, by the way. You plagiarized.'

'So?'

'Well, that's not right!' He whirled around again. 'Don't you have any standards?'

'Come on, Andy,' I said. 'It's your reputation you're worried about. If that's what really bothers you, just write one of your own.'

He raised his eyes to mine. 'You too, Gus. You can't test your theory with a plagiarized poem.'

He had me there. Clearly it had been a mistake to show it to him.

'Hang on,' I said. 'Daphne could choose from three poems. A cribbed one, one from you, and one from me.'

Andy sighed. He must have regretted ever setting foot in Jen's apartment.

'So it's on?' I asked, holding out my hand to shake on it.

He turned his back on me again.

'I'll take that as a yes.' As I turned to leave, I said, 'Why not a picture of the Sisters, then, instead of yourself?'

He didn't answer.

If this were a movie, I would now be writing the montage sequence in which the hero—Rocky, for example—would engage in extensive, inspirational training. He would be shot in a kitchen drinking raw eggs for breakfast, and then for the coup de grace, the man of the people would be shot running through the streets of Philadelphia, cheered on by his blue-collar peers.

I really can't do anything comparable. For one thing, it's not clear who the hero of this story is. It probably isn't me. Just as well: my training routine of ciggies and coffee, though effective for me personally, wouldn't make great cinema. We wrote. We ate. We made sure our paths did not cross.

Oh, Daphne and I had another session, replete with the Christmas lingerie. I suppose I should mention that.

But really, that's all that happened.

The good stuff started the next morning when it was time to hand the poems over. I knocked on Andy's door and told him his time was up. He came out and handed over his poem.

I read it quickly, greedily, a grin spreading slowly over my face as I read. I glanced up at him. He was seething.

'Dude ... it sucks. Your poem sucks!' Still looking at him, I said, 'And you know it. You *know* it's crap!'

He said nothing, just kept glaring at me, but his throat worked up and down like a short-circuited elevator.

'It's not my best,' he said, finally. His voice was stiff, on the verge of petulant. 'It's not pure,' he mumbled. 'I should never have ...' He walked away and locked himself in his room.

I was pretty chuffed. The way I saw it, I was finally on the verge of erasing the memory of that painful dinner with Jen. And, surprisingly, it'd felt good to be back in the literary saddle. I hadn't written for more than a year, but when I sat down to do it, muscle memory must have kicked in because the words flowed easily. I was really keen to get Daphne's response.

She'd arranged for us to meet at a café rather than her place. I arrived first and took a seat at a table. While I waited for her to show, I laid the poems out before me and read them over. The upbeat feeling I'd had vanished. Andy's poem might have smelt strongly of the poetic dunghill, but I'd been so carried away with my own cleverness that I couldn't see how bad my own poem was. By the time Daphne bustled into the café, desperately over-decorated with red and silver tinsel, I was feeling less than sure about the whole venture. I watched her flirt with one of the skinny-panted coffee-jerkers. I thought about nicking off and forgetting the whole ordeal, but she spotted me, trudged over, and swung into her seat. She gazed expectantly up at me.

Now call me old-fashioned, but after the amount of intimacy we'd had together, I expected at least a peck on the cheek upon arrival. But no. Today, Daphne was all business. When she saw that there were three poems, she cocked a penciled eyebrow at me.

'You inspired me,' I said, shrugging my shoulders. 'What can I say?'

'Oh, Andy,' she said. 'These are wonderful, wonderful things.'

She gazed at the poems as if they were holy relics or precious gems. Then she clasped her hands together as if she were about to start praying or give thanks and began to read the poems.

Out loud.

All I could do was wince. If I'd suspected they were bad before, Daphne giving them voice confirmed it. Their total lack of sonority and grace could not be hidden.

But Daphne didn't seem to mind.

'Andy, they're ... I don't know what to say ...' she said when she'd finished reading them. 'They're wonderful! Absolutely ...'

She'd covered her entire face with her hands now, peeking out at me from between her fingers.

'You like them?' I asked, incredulous.

She nodded.

'Well,' I said, trying to hide my surprise, 'there's a catch. You can choose only one poem.'

I wasn't sure how Daphne would respond to this, but she took it in stride. She nodded her head as if my request made all the sense in the world. I thought that I'd gotten away with it, but her face suddenly darkened.

'What if I choose the wrong one, one that won't bring Frank back? What then?'

Her lips began to quake, but then she righted herself.

'No,' she said, firmly, 'that's the old Daphne talking. Poetry is about feeling, about the senses. I'll know which one is the right one. I'll just know.'

'That's the spirit,' I said.

'Do I have to decide now, Andy?'

'Well ...'

'Oh,' she said, suddenly excited, bangles jangling, 'I'd really LOVE to read them in my Reading Corner.'

'Your what?'

At that precise moment, Daphne's apartment was being surveyed by a Feng Shui practitioner to determine the 'optimal location for creative receptivity.'

'It's probably the crapper,' I said.

She threw back her head and laughed. 'I think it's the alcove. It both receives and traps. Wherever it is, I'll call it my Reading Corner, and I'll HAVE to read your poems there.'

There was nothing I could say.

'As long as you let me know which poem you choose. That's important.'

She nodded, then turned, leaned over, and, in classic Daphne fashion, began ferreting about in her bag. I watched her fumbling hands and realized that, despite myself, I was developing a fondness for her. The café was one of those ultra-modern affairs with all the charm of a steel cube, even with their desperate attempts to be seasonal. But her presence, her dippy Daphne-quality, warmed and gave life to the place—even to the soulless electronica that beeped out of the sound system. It was a joy to watch her bring out a little red Christmas-themed notebook from her bag. It must have been scented, because the air suddenly smelt fir-tree sprucey. She took the poems one by one and filed them carefully into the notebook. I found myself smiling at her. It may have been the only genuine smile I'd had for quite a while.

I leaned across the table and tried to touch her hand, but she took hers away.

'Andy,' she said, 'we have to talk.'

I stared at her. Her tone said it all. I'd been through this so many times before that I could have completed her words for her. If she said, 'It's not you, it's me,' I think I might have screamed.

'I don't think it's right, Andy,' she said.

'Why?'

'Well, it's only cheap, meaningless sex.'

'I don't mind. Really, I don't.'

'It's beneath us, Andy. I'm sorry that I ... tempted you.'

Even while pretending to be a poet, a real published poet, I was getting dumped. Daphne explained that the Feng Shui guy would be waiting for her.

'And let me tell you,' she said, 'he isn't cheap!'

Unlike our sex, then. She gave me a quick peck on the cheek.

'So you're just going to take the poems and go?' I finally said.

'I'll see you tomorrow, Andy.'

That was fine.

Except that tomorrow never really came.

When I got back to the apartment, I found my bags packed and waiting for me at the door. Jen and her partner, Ralph, had come back early from their trip. That sniffle she'd picked up had developed into a raging flu. She lay on the couch, blasting into a tissue and clutching a hot water bottle. Andy was there too. As soon as I came in the door, I could tell from their faces and the tension in the air that Andy must have had an attack of conscience and confessed everything.

'Gus, how could you?' Jen said through a blocked nose.

She went on for quite a while. I stayed to listen. The thought went through my mind that this was indeed a low point. No one said anything else. Jen's obvious disappointment and disdain for me said all that needed to be said.

I was turfed out of the apartment—the second in a week—and probably out of Jen's life. A bridge that had been smoldering for a long time was now fully and irrevocably burnt.

You're undoubtedly thinking: so that's it? That's all? I came all this way to have Gus cop out with an unresolved ending? And not even a good one, at that? Going back to the Rocky analogy, it would be like the movie ending before you found out who won the big bout.

Well, if it's any consolation to you, that's exactly how I felt. I'd put a lot of work into the caper with Daphne, and there had been no resolution about my theory of luck and publishing.

Believe me, it ate me up.

But, befitting the season of miracles and hope, a resolution did happen. It happened by chance—or, you might say, luck.

About a week after my indecent exposure, I was wandering through Glebe. I ducked into Sappho Books and spotted Daphne at a table at the back, her nose in a book. She seemed to have ditched the 'Cross my Palm with Silver' look in favor of jeans and a jumper, but she was definitely still Daphne. She reclined with her short legs stretched out in front of her, and she held the book high up on her bosom, only inches from her face. She was totally engrossed in what she was reading. In fact, there was such an air of perfect contentment about her that I didn't want to disturb her.

But I had to find out which poem she'd chosen. A little bit tense, I walked over and greeted her.

The first thing she said was, 'How could you?'

'Well ...'

I saw in her eyes what I had done. I had genuinely hurt her, and I felt worse about it than I did about hurting Jen. Something—a nutcracker in my guts— seemed to crack inside me. I was about to explain myself, to go through the whole sorry mess of what I had done and beg forgiveness, when she said, 'Just bugger off like that? Without a word? Without a note?' She was on the verge of tears, but she fought them back. 'Did you have writing commitments?'

'Writing commitments?'

It dawned on me. They hadn't told her! For some reason, they hadn't told her. She still thought I was Andy the poet.

'Anyway, I wanted to thank you.'

'Thank me? Why?'

'For inspiring me.' She smiled.

'Sorry?' I said, totally flummoxed.

And out it came.

'You know the poems you gave me? Well, I just wasn't happy with any of them. Then I had an idea. "Daphne," I said to myself, "why don't you write your own poem? Why don't you be your own Tintoretto of the soul?" So I did. I sat in my Reading Corner all day, writing and drinking green tea. When I was done, I read all the poems over again. I decided that mine was the best.'

She was positively beaming now. In the span of two short weeks Daphne seemed to have become an entirely different person. No capes, no bangles, no headscarves. Her hair was still short and spiky but it was in what I assumed to be her natural color, a lovely chestnut brown. I hoped that she would let it grow.

'So I wanted to thank you. Without meeting you, Andy, I don't know if I ever would have written that poem.'

'So, did you give it to ... what was his name?'

'Frank?'

I nodded.

'Frack Frank!' she spat, startling me. 'I can't explain it, Andy, but once I'd finished writing the poem, I felt so certain, so sure. I was happy. Happy writing and happy being by myself. I'm going off my meds, slowly, and I'm going to get a dog, maybe a Pomeranian. I think I'll be fine. Better than ever!'

'That's great, Daphne,' I said. 'That's really great.' I actually meant it.

We chatted for a while, but I never succeeded in finding out which poem she liked best.

'They were all much of a muchness, Andy, I'm afraid,' was all she would say.

I believe that we parted as friends.

When I got home, I scribbled down the following note:

Dear Andy,
Daphne chose my poem.
Just wanted you to know.
Your mate,
Gus

I posted it to him, c/o Jen. I don't know if he ever received it.

Why didn't they tell Daphne about what I'd done? I don't really know. Probably because she seemed to have turned a corner and they didn't want to risk upsetting her. It's nice to know that maybe some good has come out of all this.

As for me, the above letter would attest that perhaps I'm not greatly changed by the whole experience. I'm still living in flats with sanctimonious roommates. But for what it's worth, I'm writing again and feeling pretty good.

Maybe, that was my Christmas gift. And maybe, just maybe, I'll have better luck this time.

Erol Engin
Bio

Originally from Toronto, Canada, Erol Engin lives and writes in Newcastle, NSW, Australia. He has been published in the Year's Best Australian Fantasy and Horror and in *Aurealis*, Australia's leading genre magazine. Other publications include stories in *Midnight Echo* (the magazine of the Australasian Horror Writers Association) and *Burial Day Books*. *The Sea Monkeys*, which appears in Papillon du Père's anthology **13 by 11**, won the Page Seventeen Short Story Contest in 2012.

Erol is currently planning and compiling an anthology of his stories, due in 2022 from Papillon du Père Publishing.

He can be contacted care of the publisher, mail@papillon-du-pere.com.

ABOUT

ST. JUDE CHILDREN'S

RESEARCH HOSPITAL

"St. Jude Children's Research Hospital, founded in 1962, is a pediatric treatment and research facility focused on children's catastrophic diseases, particularly leukemia and other cancers. The hospital costs about US$2.8 million a day to run, but patients are not charged for their care." (Wikipedia)

Find out more about them, including ways to donate, by going to https://www.stjude.org/.

St. Jude Children's®
Research Hospital
Finding cures. Saving children.

EDITOR'S
ACKNOWLEDGMENTS & THANKS

A huge thank-you to Dr. Bradley Harper for first suggesting a Christmas book in aid of St. Jude. And equally huge thank-yous to the other five authors who generously came aboard this year.

Thanks also to the marvelous Stephanie Caruso at *Paste Creative*, who enthusiastically supported this idea from its inception and continues to do so.

Thanks to my wife, Banu Özyuvacı Allchin, for her total love and support for over 18 years. It's such a cliché to talk of being *soulmates* ... but hey, that's us.

And finally, saving the best to last, many thanks to you, the reader, for stopping by and purchasing this book and thereby donating to St. Jude Children's Research Hospital. Why St. Jude? Bradley's choice. From so many one could choose. I was fully supportive that all profits go to an organization that helps children. Every child deserves a life.

As Darles Chickens famously reminds us, "For, above all, 'tis surely the season for children. For who among us deserves magic more than they?"

In these strange times, these difficult days, look after yourself, be kind, and live the good things in your life. As best you can.

Merry Christmas, Happy Holidays to one and all.

Jay Lewis Allchin

ALSO AVAILABLE FROM

PAPILLON DU PÈRE PUBLISHING

Search the author by name to find their **Amazon** page

Shea Adams

Monica Wade, Private Investigator, Mystery Series

"I was hooked from the first page. Kept me wanting more."

– Amazon review

1. **The Ashbee Cove Murders** (February 2021)

2. **The Perfect Stranger** (April 2021)

3. **The Art of Murder: The Shadowman**
(spring 2022) [expected]

4. **Who Killed Rosemary Bud?**
(fall 2022) [expected]

A series of novels featuring Monica Wade, PI, who takes the lead in dealing with danger, thugs, and murderers.

With its blend of adventure, mystery, and romance, the series is written to display warmth and wit so readers will enjoy spending time with the prime characters, Monica Wade and her best friend, the flamboyant Andy Weston.

Reminiscent of classic TV shows like *Hart to Hart*, *Remington Steele*, and *Moonlighting*.

Carla Rehse

DUSTLANDS

A near-future environmental thriller

(September 2021)

Attention all citizens. Texas is now an independent state. Remain calm. Jobs will be allotted. Resources will be allocated.

There're worse things than sleeping in a locked cellar... Some jerk breaking down the door, determined to do unholy things to my sisters and me; burying said jerk after I blow a hole through him. So, yeah, there're worse things.

Forty years after a mega-drought has wrought devastation, the USA is divided between the drought-plagued west and the flooded east. As jobs in Texas are scarcer than a dust-free day, nineteen-year-old Analee Cooper struggles to keep her younger sisters alive through her *less-than-petty* thieving. With Texas on lockdown and under martial control, Analee's testing times are just beginning ...

DUSTLANDS explores loyalty and ties against a backdrop of global warming and drought. "I wanted to create something environmentally relevant, to make people think about where the planet is headed," author Carla Rehse says. "But this is still a story about people: about family, love, what brings us together—about the lengths we'll go to protect those we love. And I get to ask to the question, *how many bad things can you do before you're no longer good?*"

"A quick-witted, timely thriller with impeccably balanced heart and grit."

– Lilla Glass
author of the forthcoming series *The Reel of Rhysia*

Papillon du Père
Anthology Collections

13 short stories by **11** award–winning
and up–and–coming authors

"*13 By 11* excels in strong images and depictions that
provide much food for thought."

– D. Donovan, senior reviewer *Midwest Book Review*

13 by 11

(September 2021)

2ⁿᵈ anthology in the **13 by 11** series

(spring 2022) [expected]

3ʳᵈ anthology in the **13 by 11** series

(fall 2022) [expected]

Thirteen short stories by **eleven** award-winning and up-and-coming authors

"An eclectic, genre-busting gathering that will appeal to a wide audience."

– D. Donovan, senior reviewer *Midwest Book Review*

Papillon du Père
Chrysalis Collection

The *Chrysalis Collection* is our literary imprint and meets our highest literary standards

Vincent Czyz

The Three Veils of Ibn Oraybi

(July 2021)

"I loved ever fluttering veil."

– Albert Goldbath, Winner of the National Book Critics Circle Award for Poetry

"Czyz weaves mystery, history, religious fervor, and social inspection into this story of struggle, which ends with a surprising twist... Its lovely, lyrical language and thought-provoking encounters not only bring the times to life but explore the politics and psychological profiles of cultures that lived side by side, but in very different worlds."

– D. Donovan, Senior Reviewer, *Midwest Book Review*

"*The Three Veils of Ibn Oraybi* is an enchantment, that rare fusion of poetry and fiction, intellectual query and sensuous revelation, narrative tension and ease of telling, that I hope for each time I open a new work. In the context of a deadly struggle between dogma and reason, it spins a tale of loyalty and betrayal in which powerless women alter the fates of powerful men. Enriched by pagan and Islamic lore, it transports the reader in fresh ways to wise places. Once I started reading it, I couldn't put it down until I finished it."

– Donald Levering, author of *Previous Lives* and winner of the Tor House Robinson Jeffers Prize in Poetry

---

All titles are available in print and on Kindle at **Amazon** and on **Barnes & Noble** Nook

PAPILLON DU PÈRE
PUBLISHING

THE
"P-DU-P CIRCLE"

Like being first in line for Xclusive stuff?*

With **P-du-P Circle**, be the first to get free books and read new excerpts.

Get *xclusive Circle discounts*, see *cover reveals*, get *release news*, *author updates*, and goodies like *free special artwork* and other bonus features like *competitions* and *author interviews* not found anywhere else.

Fancy asking your favorite P-du-P author some questions live ...? Be part of the Circle.

To join **P-du-P Circle**, just hit the mail link and add CIRCLE into your mail's subject line ...

mail@papillon-du-pere.com

That's it! **You're in.**

Look out for confirmation in you Inbox soon, and ... see you_*around*!

*Certain features coming soon

from

www.papillon-du-pere.com

@PapillonPere

www.ingramcontent.com/pod-product-compliance
Lightning Source LLC
Chambersburg PA
CBHW060917250626
47159CB00008B/3055